Katie

sprinkles

&

surprises

SIMON SPOTLIGHT

An imprint of Simon & Schuster Children's Publishing Division

1230 Avenue of the Americas, New York, New York 10020

Copyright © 2013 by Simon & Schuster, Inc.

All rights reserved, including the right of reproduction in whole or in part in any form.

SIMON SPOTLIGHT and colophon are registered

trademarks of Simon & Schuster, Inc.

Text by Tracey West

Chapter header illustrations by Emmy Reis

Designed by Laura Roode

For information about special discounts for bulk purchases, please contact

Simon & Schuster Special Sales

at 1-866-506-1949 or business@simonandschuster.com.

Manufactured in the United States of America 0115 OFF

First Edition   4 6 8 10 9 7 5 3

ISBN 978-1-4424-8590-7 (pbk)

ISBN 978-1-4424-8591-4 (hc)

ISBN 978-1-4424-8592-1 (eBook)

Library of Congress Catalog Card Number 2013950076

CUPCAKE DIARIES

Katie
sprinkles
&
surprises

by coco simon

Simon Spotlight
New York   London   Toronto   Sydney   New Delhi

CUPCAKE DIARIES

Katie
sprinkles
&
surprises

by coco simon

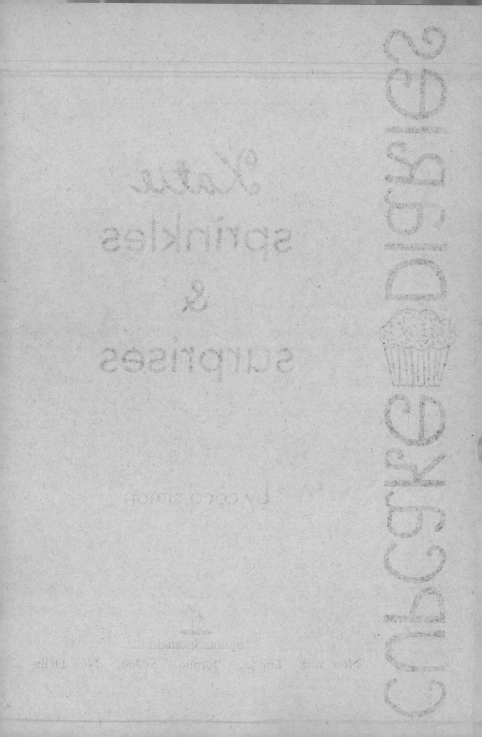

Simon Spotlight

New York   London   Toronto   Sydney   New Delhi

"Okay! Okay!" Mia got up and scooped up one wriggling dog in each arm. "Sorry, babies. Katie doesn't want to play with you."

She dropped them out the door and then shut it quickly.

"I like playing with them," I said, sitting up. "But they were attacking me."

"Those two? They're afraid of ants," Mia joked.

"They're terrors," I said. "But at least they're cute. It's too bad Mom is allergic to pets. I would love to have a dog. A big fluffy one."

Then there was a knock on the door.

"Girls, it's ice-cream time," announced Mia's stepdad, Eddie.

I smiled. "That's my favorite time of day!"

We both jumped up and followed Eddie down the stairs to the kitchen, where the table was set up for an ice-cream sundae buffet. There were three cartons of ice cream, a bottle of chocolate sauce, a can of whipped cream, and bowls filled with cherries, sprinkles, and crumbled-up cookies.

Mia's stepbrother, Dan, was leaning against the kitchen sink, eating out of a bowl that looked like it was mostly filled with whipped cream.

"What are you guys, twins?" he asked. (I forgot to mention that Dan is in high school. I have come

CHAPTER I

Mia, My Personal Adviser

$\mathcal{M}$ake them stop!" I cried, laughing. "They're tickling my nose! I'm going to sneeze!"

But my best friend, Mia, can be a little harsh sometimes. "But they *like* you!" she protested, doubled over giggling.

I was sleeping over at Mia's house, and even though she has a perfectly comfortable brand-new bed, she spread out her sleeping bag on the floor next to mine, so we could hang out and talk. But whenever anyone lies on the floor, Mia's little fluffy dogs, Tiki and Milkshake, think that it's playtime. So both of them were dancing around my face, sniffing me and licking my nose.

"Seriously, Mia!" I pleaded. "Call off your ferocious beasts!"

to believe that most high school boys are kind of rude—that's just how they are. Well, except for my friend Emma's brother Sam. He is perfect.)

Anyway, I should explain why Dan made that crack about us being twins. It's because Mia and I were wearing matching pajamas, pink ones with a cupcake pattern on them. We had bought them with the money we made from the cupcake business we're in with our friends Emma and Alexis. It's kind of funny. Any time I make money from the cupcakes, I end up spending it on something cupcake related. Last time, I got this cool stenciling kit you can use to make designs on your cupcakes. I guess you can say I am cupcake obsessed.

Mia is not as cupcake obsessed as I am, but she loved the pajamas as much as I did. And the sleepover was the perfect time to wear them.

"Yes, we're twins," Mia replied to Dan sarcastically, because apparently the best way to deal with a rude teenage boy is to be rude back. It must have worked, because Dan just shrugged and kept eating.

Eddie was anxious for us to dig in. "Come on, girls. The combination possibilities are endless!"

Mia's mom, Mrs. Valdes, entered the kitchen and gave Eddie a hug. "What a sweet thing to do, honey," she said. "Thanks!"

Mia looked at me and rolled her eyes again. I know it makes her all cringey when her mom and stepdad get lovey-dovey in front of her.

"Yes, thanks, Mr. Valdes," I said. "This looks amazing."

"What are you waiting for? Dig in before it melts!" Eddie said, motioning to us.

Mia grabbed a bowl and spoon and then stood there, thinking. I knew whatever she made would not only be the perfect balance of flavor, but also beautiful. Mia is a true artist. I'm not so picky. I took my bowl and started piling in everything.

Chocolate, mint-chip, and butter-pecan ice cream. Chocolate syrup, cookie crumbles, and cherries. Then I sprayed on the whipped cream and finally added the sprinkles.

"Katie, those sprinkles are going to fall off," Mia remarked.

"You have to put them on last," I informed her. "Because they make it pretty."

Rainbow sprinkles are my favorite because they're so colorful. Sometimes when people ask me what my favorite color is, I say "rainbow" because I just can't decide. Mom heard me say it so much that she got me rainbow socks for Christmas. They're my favorite.

4

I sat down at the table and was already halfway done eating my ice cream when Mia finally finished creating her bowl. As I predicted, it was a work of art. Mia had a perfect scoop of chocolate ice cream in her bowl, topped by a flower design painted with chocolate syrup. The center of the flower was a cherry.

"Mia, that's gorgeous!" I said.

Mia grinned. "And delicious!" Then she dug in with her spoon.

I mock screamed. "Ahh! You've destroyed it!"

"It's for a good cause," Mia said, eating another spoonful.

When we finished we helped to clean up the kitchen and then went back up to Mia's room and sprawled out on the floor again, this time without dogs.

"I'm so glad you could sleep over tonight!" Mia said. "What's your mom doing again?"

"She and her new boyfriend are going to see a Broadway show, and she won't be back till late," I said. "She figured it would be better if I slept over than if she came and got me at midnight."

"That's good, but we'll still be awake at midnight," Mia said. "Remember last time? We were up until three!"

5

I shook my head. "And then Eddie made us pancakes at, like, the crack of dawn. I was so tired!"

Then I paused. There was something I had been wanting to ask Mia.

"So, Mia, I need your advice," I began. "Of all my friends, you are the best expert on this topic."

"What topic?" Mia asked.

"Moms with boyfriends," I said. "I mean, your mom and Eddie dated for a while before they got married, right?"

Mia nodded. "Yeah."

"Was Eddie always so nice?" I asked. "For a stepdad, he seems really great."

"He is," Mia said. "But it was still weird when they started dating. I kind of kept hoping that Mom would get back together with my dad, you know?"

I nodded, but I really didn't know. Mia's mom and dad got divorced just a few years ago, but my dad left me and my mom when I was a little baby. I didn't grow up with him or anything. So there isn't any part of me that wants to see them get back together. But I could understand why Mia might feel that way.

"So, why are you asking?" Mia asked. "Because of this new boyfriend?"

"Jeff," I replied. "I haven't met him yet. All I

know about him is that he's a teacher or something, which isn't too exciting, if you ask me. And he likes to run, and he has a daughter who's younger than I am."

"Does your mom like him?" Mia asked.

"A lot, I think," I told her. "She's, like, happy all the time. She doesn't get mad anymore when I do dumb stuff, like leave my socks on the floor."

"Hmm," Mia said thoughtfully. "Mom was like that right before she and Eddie got serious."

"That's what I'm afraid of," I said. "On the drive over here she said it's time for me to meet Jeff. Like, in person!"

"How else would you meet him?" Mia asked.

"You know what I mean," I said. "Until now, he's been more of . . . an idea. But once I meet him, it will all be real."

Mia looked thoughtful. "You know, Eddie was the only boyfriend Mom ever introduced me to. I think she waited until she knew she was serious about him."

"But what about your dad?" Katie asked. "Is he serious about Lynn?"

I knew Mia's dad had been dating a woman named Lynn, who had a little boy who was kind of a pain.

"I think dads are different," Mia answered. "He's introduced me to other girlfriends before Lynn, and they didn't last. So Lynn might not last either."

"So maybe Jeff won't last?" I asked a little bit hopefully.

But Mia shook her head. "No, I'm pretty sure when moms do it, they mean it."

I groaned. "I thought so. I hope he's as nice as Eddie."

"I hope so too," Mia said. "But look on the bright side. You have the upper hand here. If you hate him, your mom is going to have a problem. If he hates you, it's his problem."

"I don't know," I said. "I'm still nervous."

Mia flopped over onto her back. "It'll work out," she said. "So, hey, did you hear about the new math teacher?"

"Oh, yeah!" I replied, quickly forgetting all about the Jeff problem. "Mr. Green, right? Everyone keeps talking about how cool he is."

"He replaced Mr. Rodriguez," Mia reported. "Mr. Rodriguez left town because his wife got a great new job in Chicago. So now Emma has Mr. Green. She says he's really funny and sweet. And I heard that at his old school, he got elected Teacher of the Year, like, five times in a row."

"Wow," I said. "Is he going to coach boys' track, too, like Mr. Rodriguez did?"

Mia nodded. "He just started. And you know what? I've heard a bunch of girls showed up to his first track practice just so they could stare at him."

"Gross! He's a teacher!" I said, making a face.

"And guess what else I heard?" Mia asked. "Olivia Allen has the biggest crush in the world on him. She's in the same class as Emma, and Emma says Olivia even goes to get extra after-school help from him even though she's pretty good at math. She's just faking it."

I shook my head. "That is so weird, but it's exactly something Olivia would do!"

Mia and I gossiped some more, and even though we stayed up late, we fell asleep just before midnight. That night I dreamed Mom took me into this white room with a door, and she said, "Katie, I'd like you to meet Jeff." And then she opened the door, and do you know what was behind it?

An ice-cream sundae with sprinkles! That's what I get for eating ice cream late at night.

CHAPTER 2

"Nice to Meet You" Cupcakes

After talking to Mia I felt a lot better about the idea of meeting Jeff in person. I was banking on the fact that if I liked him, everything would be cool, and if I didn't like him, Mom would probably dump him.

But I still wasn't prepared the next day when Mom told me she had actually set up a time for me and Jeff to meet. She broke the news on Sunday night, when we were eating Chinese food on the couch and watching shows on the food channel together.

"So," Mom said, during a commercial, "I've invited Jeff over for dinner Saturday night."

"What?" I asked, letting a forkful of cold sesame noodles fall right onto my lap.

"Like we talked about," Mom said.

"I know," I said. "It's just I didn't think it would be so soon."

Mom looked concerned. She has brown eyes like I do, and they're very expressive. It's easy to tell when she's worried or sad. "Do you really think it's too soon? Because I could cancel."

Right then I had a tough decision to make. All I had to do was say so and Mom would call it off. But I kind of felt bad for Mom. I knew she really liked Jeff. And, I mean, she hadn't had a serious boyfriend for, like, ever.

I sighed. "Saturday is okay."

Mom put her right arm across my shoulders and gave me a squeeze. "Thank you, Katie. I know you'll like him."

I didn't say anything, and the show came back on. I finished my sesame noodles and then cracked open a fortune cookie.

"Good things come to those who wait," read the fortune inside.

I looked at Mom. Was this fortune for her? I slipped the fortune into the pocket of my pajama pants.

The next day at school I decided it was time to give all my friends the Jeff details.

❁

"So, my mom is inviting her boyfriend over for dinner Saturday night so I can meet him," I blurted out at the lunch table. Sometimes it's just easier to tell people stuff that way.

"You mean Jeff?" Emma asked. She's a good listener; she always remembers every detail of every story you tell her.

I nodded. "Yeah, I might as well get it over with. But Mia made me feel better. I figure if I don't like him, Mom will break up with him."

Emma frowned. "Maybe. But didn't you see that movie on the romance network? This girl's mom had a boyfriend, and the girl didn't like him, but the mom married him anyway, and it turned out he was a secret jewel thief."

I suddenly felt worried. "I didn't see it, but it was based on a true story, right?"

Alexis interjected. "Katie, your mom is a lot smarter than that woman in the movie. If she thinks he's a nice, good guy, then you'll probably like him too. Besides, it's just one dinner. You can't let too much ride on it."

"Alexis is right, Katie. That woman in the movie was nothing like your mom," Emma agreed.

"Katie's mom is so nice," Mia remarked.

12

"Definitely," Emma said. Then her blue eyes got big. "Oh, I know. At our cupcake meeting on Thursday we should bake cupcakes for the dinner!"

"You mean, like, 'Hey Jeff, I hope you're not a creep' cupcakes?" I asked.

"More like 'Nice to meet you' cupcakes," Emma said, laughing.

"It's a good idea," Alexis said. "We have a request for strawberry cupcakes for a party in a few weeks. We can test out the recipe."

"Wait. So now Jeff is a cupcake guinea pig?" I asked. "What happened to 'Nice to meet you'?"

"He won't know the difference," Alexis pointed out. "Besides, it's the thought that counts."

"Sounds good," I said. "Text me the recipe, so I can make sure we have the ingredients."

I heard my cell phone beep in my backpack ten seconds later. Alexis is superorganized. That night Mom and I went shopping for the ingredients, and on Thursday we were ready for our cupcake meeting.

The Cupcake Club meets every Friday during school lunch, but we have to meet at other times too because business has been pretty good since we started. Alexis handles most of the business stuff because she's best at it. She keeps track of how

13

much money we earn and spend and keeps a record of our supplies and other expenses. She also makes sure our clients pay us, which is important.

Some meetings, all we do is business stuff, which is boring but important. At other meetings, we bake cupcakes for our clients or test out new cupcake recipes. It's important to try new flavors, because if you don't test them, then you won't know if they're good or not until it's too late, and all it takes is one bad batch of cupcakes for a client to ruin our business. That's why it was a good idea for us to make a batch of the strawberry cupcakes that day. And yeah, they have a mix for that, but we make our cupcakes from scratch. "From scratch" means we make everything fresh, from the beginning. That's why they're so good!

Alexis, Emma, and Mia all got to my house at five. My mom had started a batch of veggie chili in the Crock-Pot that morning, so we could all eat dinner after our meeting. We got started baking right away. My friends and I have gotten pretty good at baking together. Usually two of us work on the batter while the other two do the icing. Alexis knew the strawberry cake recipe by heart from studying it, so she and I did the batter together.

"It's not easy to get cake to taste like strawberry

without using artificial flavor," Alexis remarked. "But I think the jam in this batter is going to be nice."

"And using homemade strawberry syrup to flavor the icing will really taste good," I added.

Mia was stirring the strawberries, water, and sugar on top of the stove while Mom supervised.

"It smells awesome," Mia reported.

The strawberry syrup cooled while we baked the cupcakes in the oven. Then Mia and Emma mixed the syrup in the blender with butter and powdered sugar to make the frosting. When the cupcakes were done, we had to wait for them to cool before we iced them, so Mom spooned us bowls of veggie chili. Mia and I put sliced jalapeños on top of ours, because we like things spicy. After the chili, we iced the cupcakes.

"They look so pretty," Emma said admiringly.

"The client wants pink flowers on top, but you can work on that, right, Mia?" Alexis asked.

Mia nodded. "No problem." She designs most of our cupcake decorations.

"These look great, but they're kind of boring for 'Nice to meet you' cupcakes," I said.

Mom smiled. "Oh? Who are these for?"

"We thought we could use some for our dinner

with Jeff," I said, and Mom looked like she might burst with happiness.

"Oh, that's so sweet of all of you," she said, beaming. "Thank you! He will love them."

"I hope he likes pink," Alexis said.

"If he doesn't like pink, then he's just not a good boyfriend," I announced, which made no sense at all if you think about it. But Mom didn't look worried. "Anyway, I still think they look boring."

Then I remembered the sleepover with Mia and had an idea. I ran into the kitchen closet and came out with a container of rainbow sprinkles.

"These make everything better," I said with a grin, and I grabbed a spoon and started sprinkling the cupcakes.

Alexis shook her head. "You are rainbow crazy."

"Sprinkles are great," Mia said. "They cover up any mess you make with the icing."

"And they're pretty besides!" I added.

When we were done, we had a plate of very cheerful cupcakes. We stood back and admired our work.

"If Jeff doesn't like these, then he has no soul!" I said.

CHAPTER 3

Olivia, the Lovesick Puppy

The next day I brought four of the "Nice to meet you" cupcakes to school for our Friday Cupcake Club meeting. It's been a tradition since we started—every Friday is Cupcake Friday! (Although Mia has often suggested we move it to Monday, since she hates Mondays and she thinks cupcakes would make them better—which they would. But it's hard to break a tradition once you start it.)

Sometimes it's tempting to dig in to the cupcakes before we eat lunch, but we have learned to restrain ourselves. Besides it's more fun to "save the best for last." So as we ate our lunches, Alexis went over cupcake business with us.

"I have some exciting news," she announced. "I got an e-mail last night from a brand-new client. The director of the Maple Grove Children's Museum wants us to bake cupcakes for the opening of a space exhibit there next month."

"Outer space?" I asked. "Cool! We could do cupcakes with alien faces."

"Or cupcakes that look like planets," Mia suggested.

Emma looked thoughtful. "What kinds of flavors can you do for outer space?" she wondered out loud.

"How about . . . green cheese, for the moon?" I exclaimed.

"Ew!" all my friends said at once.

"But we use cream cheese in cupcakes all the time," I pointed out.

Before we could discuss green cheese cupcakes any more, Mia suddenly pointed. "Oh my gosh! Look at Olivia. She's trailing after Mr. Green like a lost puppy."

Mr. Green, the new math teacher everyone was talking about, was monitoring the lunchroom that day, because all the teachers take turns. I guess it wasn't his first time doing it because he seemed really comfortable. He was walking among the tables, making sure everyone was eating and cleaning up after themselves and not throwing food and being jerks. Some teachers walk around with a mean face on, but Mr. Green was smiling and chatting with people.

Mia was right about Olivia; she was two steps behind him, and it looked like she was trying to offer him an apple from her lunch.

"Oh my gosh, that is hilarious!" Alexis said. "She is making a fool of herself!"

That may sound mean, but I guess we have some issues with Olivia. When she was new in school, Mia had become friends with her. But Olivia totally used Mia and then dumped her so she could be a part of the BFC, the Best Friends Club. She also did a bunch of other stuff to Mia that wasn't very nice. So if Alexis was going to point out that Olivia was making a fool of herself, I wasn't going to stop her.

Emma sort of defended her. "Lots of girls have crushes on Mr. Green," she said (and the way she said it, I wondered if she did too). "You have to admit, he's really gorgeous."

"I guess," I said. Mr. Green has wavy brown hair and nice green eyes. (Mr. Green with green eyes! No wonder.) "But he's a teacher! Ew!"

"Ew!" Mia agreed. "I mean, he seems really awesome, but I could never think of a teacher as gorgeous. That's just weird."

Then Alexis quickly nudged her. Mr. Green was walking up to *our* table.

"Hello, girls," he said. Then his eyes landed on the see-through cupcake carrier on the table. "Hey, I've heard about the Cupcake Club. Your cupcakes are legendary."

"Thanks," Emma said, and I saw she was blushing a little. "Would you like one?"

Mr. Green held up his hands. "No, but thank you. I see there are just enough for the four of you. Guess I'll have to hire you for something if I'm going to get to taste one."

Alexis whipped out a business card faster than a cowboy drawing his gun in a shoot-out.

"We do custom orders," she said, handing him the card. "No order is too big or too small."

Mr. Green laughed. "Good to know. Thanks." And then he headed to the next table.

Mia leaned in. "I bet Olivia is so jealous right now! What do you want to bet she'll bring him a cupcake on Monday?"

"She can bring in all the cupcakes she wants, but they won't be as good as ours," Alexis said confidently.

"Well, anyway, I guess I can see why everyone likes him," I said. "He seems nice. And, hey, it's pretty cool he's heard about the Cupcake Club already. I mean, he's only been here, like, a week, right? We must be famous."

"Not famous enough, if you ask me," Alexis said. She looked through her notebook. "Well, I think that's all the new business for now. We should all think of ideas for the space exhibit, though."

I nodded. "No problem. I'll probably want to live in outer space after I meet Jeff tomorrow."

"Don't worry, Katie," Mia said. "I have a feeling it will go just fine."

"I hope so," I said, but the more I thought about it, the more the meeting with Jeff felt like a big deal.

CHAPTER 4

I Wasn't Expecting That!

The day of the big "meet and greet," I started to clean my room like crazy. I don't think in the history of my life I have ever cleaned up my room without my mom telling me to, but I guess I was nervous or something. So that's why I was hanging upside down over my bed, pulling out dirty socks covered with dust bunnies from underneath.

"Gross!" I squealed, removing a sock so covered with dust that I couldn't tell what color it was originally. I tossed it into my laundry basket, shuddering.

After I got all my dirty clothes off the floor, I glanced at the clock: 5:50. Ten more minutes until Jeff showed up. This was more suspenseful than on those reality shows, when they make you wait until after the commercial to tell you who gets voted off. I was still really nervous, so I sent a text to Mia, Emma, and Alexis:

Jeff will be here in 10! Freaking out!

Mia replied first.

Don't freak. Go to ur happy place.

My happy place is an imaginary room filled with shelves of delicious cupcakes, comfy beanbag chairs shaped like cupcakes, and cupcake recipe books to read while you're eating. I closed my eyes and tried to go there, but then my phone made a twinkly noise. I had another text.

He will be nice, Emma texted. I can feel it.

And there was a text from Alexis, too.

Be calm. Nothing big will happen 2nite.

Alexis had a point. This was just a meeting.

Tx guys! I texted back.
Full report when you're done, Alexis typed.
K, I replied.

23

I closed my eyes again, so I could try to go to my happy place, but then the doorbell rang downstairs. I didn't move, though. I sat very still on my bed, listening to the muffled voices coming from the front door. Then Mom yelled, "Katie!"

I took a deep breath. For a split second I considered climbing out my window, but I knew that was ridiculous. How bad could this guy be, anyway?

I slowly made my way down the stairs. The voices were coming from the kitchen now, and I could hear Mom laughing.

Jeff must make her really happy, I thought, not for the first time. So the least I could do was try to like him, right?

I slowly peeked into the kitchen. Mom was at the stove, stirring a pot of spaghetti sauce, and Jeff was sitting at the kitchen table, although I couldn't see him yet. I kind of had to take in the whole scene for a minute. I couldn't help wondering: If Mom married Jeff, is this what it would be like? The two of them together, laughing and talking, while I watched from the sidelines? It was a depressing thought.

Then Mom's mom-radar kicked in, and she looked up and saw me by the door.

24

"Oh, there you are, Katie!" she said. "Come meet Jeff."

I stepped into the kitchen and walked up to the kitchen table. Sitting there was . . . Mr. Green! The *math* teacher! For a second I was confused.

"Mr. Green?" I asked. Had Mom hired him to tutor me in math or something?

Mr. Green laughed. "You can call me Jeff when we're out of school, Katie," he said. "Nice to meet you officially. Your mom has told me all about you."

Then it really, actually hit me. Mr. Green and Jeff were the same person! My mom was dating Mr. Green, the math teacher at school who everyone liked! Not only that, but he said *Your mom has told me all about you.* Which means, when he came up to our table the other day, he knew who I was, but I didn't know who *he* was. That didn't seem fair at all. I felt pretty mad at my mom at that point, but I tried not to show it.

"Um, that's nice," I said.

"Katie, can you please set the table for us?" Mom asked.

"Sure," I replied. Our house is kind of small, so we don't have a dining room, like at Mia's house. We eat in the kitchen, which can be pretty cozy. Although right then it was feeling a little bit crowded.

I opened the cabinet to take out the plates, and Mr. Green–Jeff jumped right up.

"Let me help you with that, Katie," he said.

"No, it's all right," I told him. I didn't like the idea of him setting the table, like he was part of the house—part of the family. So I quickly set the table by myself, and soon we were all seated while Mom passed around the salad bowl.

"Mmm, this looks great, Sharon," Jeff said. "Lots of veggies!" And then he and my mom both said, at the same time, "Five a day!" and then laughed.

It was like they had known each other for a million years. I stayed quiet at first, mostly because I wanted to watch the two of them together, but also because Jeff didn't ask me a bunch of dumb questions about how I liked school and stuff, like most adults do when they meet you for the first time. Then Jeff started talking about this family of geese that lives at the park in town. I know about them because Mom and I see them when we go running together.

"So I was running by myself the other morning," Jeff said, "and then I heard a noise behind me, and the mother goose was chasing me! And then

26

all her little goslings started following her!"

"Did they catch up to you?" I asked.

"I lost them on the blue trail," Jeff replied. "And it's a good thing, too, because that mom looked like she wanted to feed me to her babies!"

I laughed. "She gets very upset if you run too close," I said, and then I noticed a pleased look on Mom's face, like she was happy Jeff and I were talking. Which for some reason just made me want to get quiet again, so I did.

The rest of the dinner was pretty much okay. Mom had made her spaghetti Bolognese, which has this delicious meat sauce on it, and Jeff was funny and easy to talk to. I could understand why everyone thought he was a great teacher, and also why Mom liked him.

When we were done eating, Jeff insisted on clearing off the table. "I want to make room for your secret weapon, Katie," he said. "The cupcakes! I've been saving room for days."

I looked at my mom, and then at Jeff, and then it clicked. "Oh, I get it," I said. "That's why yesterday in the lunchroom you said you knew all about the Cupcake Club."

"Well, a lot of the other teachers talk about your cupcakes," Jeff informed me. "But I did get the full story from your mom."

I wanted to say, *Gee, it's nice that* somebody *around here got the full story*, but I kept my mouth shut. Mom really hates when I'm sarcastic, and besides, I didn't want to ruin things for her. Even though I was mad at Mom for telling him all about me and not telling me anything, it was hard not to like Jeff.

So instead I said, "I'll get the cupcakes," and then I fetched them from the pantry. Jeff looked really happy when I put the plate on the table.

"Oh, yeah, these are the ones you had yesterday," he said. "Awesome! I love sprinkles."

He took a bite of one. "Wow, these are even better than they look!" he said. "You are a cupcake wizard, Katie."

"Thanks," I replied. He might have been saying that just to be nice, but then again he did eat three whole cupcakes, all by himself. So I think he meant it.

"Katie, would it be okay if I took one home for my daughter?" he asked.

My ears perked up a little. Mom did say Jeff had a daughter.

"Sure," I said. "What's her name?"

"Emily," Jeff replied. "She's two years younger

than you are. She likes to read, and she also likes to run with me."

"You have a lot in common!" Mom interjected, beaming.

I had to try really hard not to roll my eyes. Reading and running are just two things. I wouldn't call that a *lot* in common. But I kept that thought to myself.

As I packed up two cupcakes for Emily (one extra, to be nice), I thought about what it might be like to have a little sister around. I have this weird thing with kids. I'm really good at playing with them and stuff, but I have to warm up to it. I've been an only child for so long that sometimes being around kids stresses me out.

Then I thought about my friends. Emma has a younger brother, Jake, who is adorable, but Emma says he can be a pain a lot of the time. Alexis has an older sister, Dylan, who is totally rude to her most of the time, but every once in a while she helps Alexis with stuff. But Emily is not a teenager, and she's not a little kid, like Jake. So maybe having a little sister Emily's age would be all right.

I handed Jeff a little box with the cupcakes in it, thinking he was leaving. But then Mom said, "I thought we could all watch that movie about the girl who saved those dolphins. It's just out on cable."

By "all," Mom obviously meant to include Jeff. I wasn't sure how I felt about that. Usually when Mom and I watch a movie together at night, we change into our pajamas, but no way was I going to do that with Jeff there. Me in my pajamas in front of Mr. Green? That would be too weird.

"Um, okay," I said, and Mom grinned.

"Great! I'll make popcorn."

The good thing about watching the movie was we didn't have to talk to one another. The bad thing was that I sat in the blue armchair, which is my favorite, and Mom sat on the couch with Jeff, and halfway through the movie I looked over and saw they were holding hands. Ew!

So I was relieved when the movie ended and Jeff got up and stretched and said, "I should be going. It's late. Thank you both for a lovely time."

"Good night," I said, and then I went upstairs as Mom walked Jeff to his car. I'm sure they kissed each other good night, but I did not want to be around to witness that.

While I was brushing my teeth, Mom opened the bathroom door.

"So what do you think of Jeff?" she asked. I could tell she'd been waiting all night to ask me.

I was so tired, and I didn't really feel like talking about it. "He's nice, Mom," I said. "But I already knew that from school."

I knew Mom was waiting for me to bring up the fact that Jeff was also Mr. Green, the math teacher, and she was dying to talk about it. But I didn't give her a chance.

"I'm really tired, Mom," I said, and then I gave her a kiss on the cheek and went into my room. Mom didn't push it.

When I got into bed I saw that my cell phone was lighting up with texts.

So what happened? Is he nice? Mia asked, and Emma and Alexis basically wrote the same thing.

I didn't want to ignore my friends, but I didn't feel like breaking the big news about Mr. Green just yet, either. So I shut off the phone and closed my eyes.

As I drifted off to sleep, crazy thoughts started popping into my head. Mom and Jeff seemed like a great couple. What if they got married? Would I have to share my room with Emily? That would be hard, because my room is pretty small.

Then I had another thought: Maybe Jeff had a

bigger house, and he would want us to live with him. Mia and her mom moved in with Eddie, so it was entirely possible. I looked around my room, and even in the dark I could make out the lightning bolt–shaped crack in my ceiling and saw the soft glow of the star stickers on my unicorn poster. I loved my room. I didn't want to leave.

Change stinks, I thought, and then I tossed and turned until I finally fell asleep.

CHAPTER 5

Mom Is Totally Clueless

When I woke up the next morning there was a text from Mia.

Dying for details.

Somehow I still couldn't break the news that Jeff and Mr. Green were the same person—not even to my best friend.

L8r. At the cc mtg, I typed back.

Aaargh! Suspense! Mia replied, but she didn't push it after that, and I was grateful.

Then I went downstairs, where Mom was sitting at the kitchen table, sipping coffee and reading the paper. I didn't see any breakfast on the table, so I went to the pantry and got a box of cereal.

"So, Katie, I think we should talk about last night" were the first words out of Mom's mouth. Not "Good morning" or "How did you sleep?" or "Are you hungry?"

"Mm-hmm," I mumbled, annoyed.

"I thought things went really well," Mom went on.

"Yup," I said, avoiding her gaze. I got the milk out of the fridge next.

Mom sighed. "Okay, Katie, use your words. What's bothering you?"

I put the milk carton on the table in front of her. "Okay. It's just . . . I can't believe you didn't tell me that Jeff is Mr. Green! That he's a teacher in my school!"

Mom nodded. "I understand. But we wanted to wait until the two of you met officially. And it's all very new. When I first started dating Jeff, he was teaching in another school. The switch to your school was pretty sudden."

"It's not fair," I said. "You still knew he was in my school. And it's like he knew who I was before I knew who he was. Plus, what if you guys get married and we have to move into his house? I don't want to leave my room. I like this house. And Emily sounds nice and all, but what if I don't want a little sister?"

Mom's eyes got big. "Whoa," she said. "First of all, nobody is talking about getting married right now, so slow down."

I sat down in my chair while Mom continued. "Secondly, nobody's talking about moving right now either."

"Good."

"But I'll be honest, Katie, I really like Jeff, and he likes me," Mom said. "Our relationship is getting serious, I guess. But if we ever did decide to . . . make things permanent, I promise you we won't make any fast decisions. We'd all talk about things together, okay?"

"Okay," I said. "But you still should have told me Jeff was Mr. Green."

"I wanted to first make sure that you weren't in his class, because that might cause some issues," Mom answered. "But you aren't."

I looked at Mom. She is a very smart woman— she's a dentist! But right now she sounded pretty clueless.

"Don't you see?" I said. "If you're dating one of the teachers in my school, it's going to be weird, period. It doesn't matter if I'm in his class or not."

Mom looked thoughtful. "I see your point. But if it does become an issue, we'll deal with it together, okay? I always want you to feel like you can come talk to me, Katie. Especially about stuff like this."

"Sure," I said with a sigh. Mom just didn't get it. She was dating Mr. Green. I didn't have to wait for it to become an issue—it already was an issue!

Mom went back to reading her paper, and I got to thinking as I ate my cereal. Mom had been dating Jeff for a while, and so far nobody knew he was Mr. Green but me. The best thing I could do was to keep it a secret—even from my friends—and then maybe, maybe, I could get through the rest of the school year.

I hated not telling them, but it was my only hope for a normal life. At least that's what I thought, anyway.

CHAPTER 6

More Developments in Awkwardness

The Cupcake Club had a meeting on Sunday afternoon, after Mia got back from visiting her dad. Remember I told you her parents are divorced too? Well, Mia spends every other weekend with her dad in Manhattan, in the apartment she grew up in. I always miss her when she's gone.

Mom dropped me off at Emma's house at two o'clock.

"I'll pick you up at five," she said. "Jeff and I are going for a run, but I have my cell phone if you need me."

"Say hi to *Mr. Green* for me," I said. I wasn't ready to let Mom forget she was dating a teacher in my school. I smirked at her.

Mom had on her patient face. "I will."

When I got out of the car, Emma was chasing her little brother, Jake, across the lawn.

"Hey, Katie!" she said. She grabbed Jake and hugged him. "Tag! You're it! Except I need to start my meeting now."

"But I'm it!" Jake protested. "So you'd better run!"

Emma shook her head, but she ran inside, and I followed them into Emma's kitchen. Jake was hanging off her arm.

"You're it now! Chase me! Chase me!"

Emma sighed. "Stop it, Jake."

"But you're it!" her little brother wailed.

Emma rolled her eyes. "Mom! Tell Jake to quit bugging me, please! Katie is here!" she yelled.

Mrs. Taylor came into the kitchen. "Emma, please don't yell," she scolded. Then she smiled at me. "Hi, Katie."

"Hi, Mrs. Taylor," I said. Emma's mom is the only one in their whole family without blond hair. Hers is brown, like mine.

"Mia and Alexis will be here any minute," Emma said. "Jakey, we need to work now, okay?"

Mrs. Taylor grabbed Jake's hand. "Come on,

Jakey. Let's go play ball in the yard."

"I get to lick the bowl!" Jake cried over his shoulder as Mrs. Taylor pulled him outside.

Then Emma and I were alone in the kitchen. I knew she was going to ask about Jeff, so I quickly brought up another topic.

"So, how was your modeling job yesterday?" I asked. Emma has a lot of stuff going on. Besides being in the Cupcake Club, she plays the flute, has a dog-walking business, and even does modeling on the weekends sometimes.

"Kind of fun," Emma replied. "I had to model clothes for a winter catalog for this store, and it was superhot in the studio, but I had to wear a fuzzy parka! I was sweating like crazy."

I laughed. "I never thought about that before. I think I have a new respect for models."

Then Alexis and Mia came into the kitchen.

"Your dad let us in," Alexis reported.

"Emma was just telling me about her modeling job," I said quickly, before Alexis and Mia could start firing Jeff questions. That worked for, like, a minute, but then Mia was in the chair next to me, her eyes shining with curiosity.

"So, what's Jeff like?" Mia asked.

I took a deep breath. I could tell the truth

without telling the whole story.

"He's nice," I said. "And funny, and my mom really likes him."

"What does he look like?" Alexis asked.

I had to be careful about this one. "Regular, I guess. Brown hair. He has a daughter, and she's, like, two years younger than I am. So if Mom and Jeff get married, I'll have a younger sister."

"That's definitely better than getting stuck with an older sister," Alexis said, making a face.

"Or a little brother," Emma added. "Or even an older brother. I've always wanted a sister."

"And she's only two years younger," Mia pointed out. "She's not some gross little kid."

"You mean like Ethan?" I asked.

Mia nodded. "Yesterday he insisted on making his own lunch, and he made the drippiest peanut-butter-and-jelly sandwich ever. Every time he took a bite, jelly squirted onto his shirt. And his hands were sticky and gross all day long."

"Eww!" I squealed, along with Alexis and Emma.

"Can we please stop talking about this and make some cupcakes?" Alexis asked. "We've got to get this birthday order done."

"Let's do it," I said quickly. Everyone seemed to

have forgotten about Jeff, which was good.

We had a birthday order for two dozen cupcakes that was due by six o'clock that night. We were cutting it kind of close, but Mia was with her dad yesterday and Emma had her modeling thing.

I started chopping up apples for the batter, Emma started mixing the dry ingredients, Alexis whipped up a cream cheese frosting, and Mia started working on the decorations. Not only would the cupcakes be apple flavored, but they would look like apples too, with red icing, green leaves cut from fruit rolls, and a skinny pretzel stick for a stem.

"Is this red enough?" Alexis asked, holding up the bowl of icing she'd been working on.

"Add a little more gel," I suggested. Getting icing to look really red is hard to do with regular food coloring, but we found a gel that works pretty well. Alexis nodded and went back to work.

Before long the cupcakes were out of the oven, and the whole house smelled like apples and cinnamon. That's when Emma's brother Matt came into the kitchen. He's a year older than we are, and he's got blond hair and blue eyes, like Emma. He could probably be a model too, but he'd rather play sports—all of them.

41

"I'm ready to help," he said.

Emma snorted. "Yeah, you mean you're here to eat a cupcake."

"Hey, it's an important job," Matt said. "You need me to test the cupcakes for you."

Alexis handed him a freshly iced cupcake. "Here you go."

"Thanks," Matt said, and then he took a bite. "Shish ish really good," he said with his mouth full.

"Thanks," Emma said, rolling her eyes.

Then I had a sort of reverse thought. Emma and Alexis were always complaining about their older siblings. What if Emily met me and she didn't like *me*? I mean, I couldn't imagine being annoying to anybody, but it was possible.

"You need to get out of here," Emma told Matt. "We have more cupcake business to discuss."

"Matt can stay," Alexis said. (She has a little bit of a crush on him.)

Matt smiled at Alexis, then looked at Emma. "I'll leave, but it'll cost you," he said, holding out his hand.

Emma put another cupcake onto his palm. "Now, go!"

Alexis looked a little disappointed, but she got over it quickly, because now she could discuss cupcake business, which she loves doing.

"So we should talk about the job for the children's museum," Alexis said as she continued icing the apple cupcakes. "Mia, did you ask your dad about that weekend?"

Mia sighed. "I asked him, but he says it's his time with me, and he has something planned. So I can design the cupcakes and the display, but I can't be around to make them or deliver them. Sorry."

"That's too bad," Emma said worriedly. "You're usually around when we do the fancy cupcakes. You're the best at it."

"Aww, thanks, Emma," Mia said. "I love decorating our cupcakes! I am really sorry."

"As long as we prepare correctly, everything will go smoothly," Alexis said. "Mia, you can write up detailed instructions for us and even do a demo before the event."

Mia nodded. "Of course! Anything! I know this is a big job."

"Also, I spoke with the director of the children's museum," Alexis reported. "She wants to meet us on Saturday morning to go over what they want. We can walk around and get some ideas for how to do the display."

"Perfect! I can be there!" Mia promised.

Emma frowned. "That's the day we deliver the mini cupcakes to The Special Day. But you guys can go, and I'll make the delivery. Mona wants me to model some bridesmaid dresses that day, anyway." (I forgot to mention—that's another thing Emma does. She helps us with our gig making mini cupcakes for a bridal shop.)

"No problem," Alexis said. "When we're busy like this, it makes sense to split up. I'll text you guys with the details, and we can figure out who'll drive us for the meeting."

At that moment my phone made a noise, and there was a text from my mom saying she was outside.

"I've got to go," I said. "Thanks for handling the birthday delivery, Alexis."

"No problem," Alexis said.

I went outside and got into the car.

"How was your run?" I asked.

"Nice," Mom said. Then she casually added, "So, I was talking to Jeff about the Wilsons' party."

"You were?" I asked, confused, and I should probably explain why. Since I was a little kid, my mom and I have been friends with the Wilsons. I used to be best friends with Callie Wilson, until she dumped me at the beginning of middle school.

That was painful, but now we are okay with each other, I guess. It's still a little awkward any time we're together. Anyway, Callie's mom was having a birthday party next week, and Mom and I were invited.

Mom nodded. "So, I thought it would be nice if Jeff came with us."

I let that statement hang in the air for a minute. Mom wanted to bring Jeff to Callie's house. Callie would know Jeff was Mr. Green. Talk about awkward! And so much for keeping Mr. Green a secret.

"But I was trying to . . . ," I began, but I didn't finish. Callie's mom was still Mom's best friend. Callie was going to find out sooner or later.

"What, Katie?" Mom asked. "Don't you think it will be fun to have Jeff with us?"

"It's not that," I said. "It's just really awkward, you know?"

"It'll be fine, Katie," Mom said. "The Wilsons are like family."

It'll be fine. That was Mom's answer for everything these days. I just wished I could believe her.

Woo-hoo!

CHAPTER 7

I Can't Believe I Said That!

All week during school I tried to avoid Mr. Green. It was kind of easy, because I don't have him for a teacher. But he had lunchroom duty on Friday again, and he came over to our table. I tried to act natural, but my palms were all sweaty.

"Hello, Cupcake Club," he said in that friendly way of his.

Alexis held up a paper holder with a cupcake in it. "I brought in an extra one for you," she said.

Mr. Green's eyes lit up. "Why, thank you, Alexis," he said. Then he took a bite right in front of us. "Mmm, so good!"

Fortunately, a table of boys started getting really loud across the room, so Mr. Green had to go.

"Why did you bring him an extra cupcake?" I

asked Alexis when Mr. Green was out of earshot. I wasn't accusing her; I was just curious.

"I bet she has a crush on him," Emma said with a giggle.

"Of course not!" Alexis said. "I just wanted to see what Olivia's reaction would be. And it's priceless."

She made a slight nod to the Best Friends Club table, and sure enough, Olivia was glaring at us with narrowed eyes.

"Just as I thought," Alexis said, pleased. "She's jealous!"

"That's just silly," I said. To be honest, I didn't like all the attention Mr. Green was getting. Besides making me nervous, it was just weird, considering he was dating my mom. So I quickly changed the subject. (I've been getting good at that, if you haven't noticed.)

"So my mom says she'll drive us to the museum tomorrow morning," I said. "Around ten?"

"Sounds good," Alexis said, immediately typing the info into her phone.

"Sounds early," Mia said with a little groan.

"Let me know what happens," Emma joined in.

I was kind of glad we had the museum appointment on Saturday, because it took my mind off Callie's party on Sunday, when the whole

Mr. Green secret was going to blow wide open.

As Alexis and Mia and I rode to the museum the next day, I thought about telling them, but I couldn't bring myself to do it. For one thing, my mom was in the car, and it would have been awkward. But, also, I was kind of hoping I could still keep the secret. Callie was always good at keeping secrets when we were little. But mostly I guess I just didn't want to deal with it.

Anyway, I forgot all about Mr. Green–Jeff when we pulled up to the museum. It had only been open for a couple of years, so I was sort of too old to go when it opened. But secretly I thought it looked like a lot of fun. The museum is in an old building downtown that used to be a bank or something, I think. On the front of the building, the words MAPLE GROVE CHILDREN'S MUSEUM were spelled out in these colorful 3-D letters. In the front window there was a display with this big, purple cardboard monster with a huge wide-open mouth, and a cardboard kid was throwing bottles and cans into it. A sign underneath read, TAME THE GARBAGE MONSTER! COME SEE OUR RECYCLING EXHIBIT!

We stepped inside the doorway, and the place was filled with screaming kids. To be fair, there were also a lot of them quietly exploring the museum. In the front room there was this whole cool display about the water cycle, and across the room was this tube where you could talk on one end and someone could hear your voice all the way on the other end. But a lot of the kids were just running around and acting crazy.

"Is this where the space exhibit is going to be?" Mia wondered.

"I wish we were in space now," I said. "I bet it would be easier dealing with evil aliens than dealing with all these kids."

"I don't know. I think those two kids are kind of cute."

Now, you might think Alexis or Mia or even my mom said that. But it wasn't any of them. I turned around, and to my surprise I saw George Martinez, standing behind me. I have known George since elementary school, and we both like each other— you know, *like* each other. If there's a school dance, George dances with me, and sometimes he invites me to hang out after school with him and some of our other classmates. But he's not my boyfriend or anything.

"Oh, hi, George," I said, and then I noticed the two little boys he was pointing at. They were about four years old, but they looked like mini versions of George. Then it hit me: Those were the twins George's mom used to push in a stroller when she picked up George from elementary school. They were George's brothers—and I had just insulted them!

"Your brothers are definitely cute," I said, mortified, and then I scrambled to explain myself. "It's just there's a ton of kids here, and they're, like, crazy, you know? But not your brothers. They're not crazy."

Then George's brothers ran past us, screaming loudly, and George laughed.

"It's okay," he said. "Sometimes I wish they were aliens too."

I laughed, relieved, and then I saw a woman with short dark hair approaching us. She wore jeans, a red sweater, and a colorful beaded necklace. I recognized her right away. It was George's mom. I figured Mrs. Martinez and George were there with the twins, having fun, but I was wrong.

Alexis walked right up and shook her hand. "Hello, Mrs. Martinez," she said. "I'm Alexis Becker. We spoke on the phone."

"Alexis, very nice to meet you," Mrs. Martinez said. Then she nodded to me and Mia. "And you must be the other members of the Cupcake Club.

Of course I know you, Katie. George talks about you all the time. How is your mom?"

"She's here, actually, looking around," I told her. "She's driving us here—I mean, she drove us here."

I was mixing up my words because I was nervous. First, because I had just figured out George's mom was the director of the children's museum, the person who had hired us. Second, because she said George talked about me all the time. What did he say? And why was she smiling at me like that?

"I'll be sure to say hi to her before you leave," said George's mom. "Let's meet in my office, where it's quieter. George, please watch your brothers."

"Isn't that what I always do?" George asked. Then he waved to me as my friends and I followed Mrs. Martinez through the museum.

George's mom gave us a tour as we walked. "On the second floor is our music center," she said. "And our playroom is back here, next to the party room. That's where you'll be setting up the cupcakes."

The playroom was supercool, with a tiny little grocery store, fire station, and school. And it opened up to a sunny room with bright yellow walls and a big long table with chairs around it.

"This is the room we usually use for birthday parties," Mrs. Martinez explained. "You can push that table against the wall for your display, and we'll put the chairs away for the event, so people will have room to walk around."

Mia started sketching the room on her pad. "Then you'll need a really big display, so people can see the cupcakes through the crowd."

"That would be nice," Mrs. Martinez said. "Did you have any ideas yet?"

"We were hoping to learn more about the space exhibit first," Alexis replied.

Mrs. Martinez nodded. "I have lots of pictures. Follow me."

She led us through a door marked STAFF and into a narrow hallway, then into her office. I noticed a nice picture of George and his brothers on her desk, and on the wall was a cool poster of outer space, and it said, SHOOT FOR THE MOON. EVEN IF YOU MISS, YOU'LL LAND AMONG THE STARS.

Mrs. Martinez sat at her desk and swung her monitor toward us so we could see. There was a picture of a room with models of the planets hanging from the ceiling, and a rocket ship that kids could climb around in.

"We're modeling the exhibit on this one," she said, "but we'll be adding some things too."

"It's very science-y," Mia remarked. "Do you

want the cupcakes to be science-y too? Or can we do alien faces and stuff like that?"

"I think it's okay to get a little fantastic with the cupcakes," Mrs. Martinez replied. "But maybe it would be nice if the cupcake display could reflect the exhibit somehow too."

Mia nodded and wrote down some notes in her sketchbook. She and Alexis are always prepared like that. I was starting to get some ideas, but I had no place to put them.

"What about flavors?" I asked. "Do you want us to come up with some space themed ones?"

"I think maybe it's safest to stick with vanilla and chocolate," she replied. "But if you girls come up with something special, feel free to pass it by me."

"We'll e-mail you," Alexis said, and then she handed Mrs. Martinez a piece of paper. "Here's a copy of your order. Please look it over and sign it if you approve."

"My, you girls are professional," Mrs. Martinez said with a smile that showed she was pleased and not annoyed by that fact. She put on a pair of glasses to read it, and a minute later she signed it.

"I'll send you a copy," Alexis said.

Mrs. Martinez stood. "Thank you so much for

coming, girls. It's a relief to know the refreshments will be in good hands."

"You won't be disappointed," Alexis promised, and I hoped she was right. It's one thing to disappoint a client, but I really didn't want to disappoint George's mom!

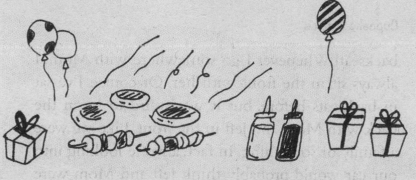

CHAPTER 8

Not So Bad After All . . .

Good morning, Katie. Good morning, Sharon."

Mr. Green–Jeff (I guess I'll call him Jeff when it's not school) picked up Mom and me the next day at noon. It was warm out, so he was wearing shorts and a green collared shirt and loafers. It's weird seeing a teacher in shorts. You just don't expect it.

"Good morning," I said.

Jeff looked at his watch. "Actually, it's 12:01, so I guess I should say 'Good afternoon.'"

Mom kissed him. "It's good to see you, no matter what time it is."

Gross! Now I knew how Mia felt when her mom and Eddie got all sappy with each other.

Then we walked to Jeff's car and loaded the food we had made, and I got in the backseat. The backseat! Whenever I go somewhere with Mom, I always sit in the front with her. Of course I've sat in backseats before, but it was weird to be in the back with Mom and Jeff in the front. Like we were a family or something. In fact, anyone looking into our car would probably think Jeff and Mom were my parents and I was their kid. Weird!

Callie doesn't live far away, so luckily it was a short ride, because I didn't feel like talking. Mom must have tipped off Jeff that I was worried about the party, because he kept joking around to lighten the mood.

"Cheer up, Katie!" he said, looking at me in the rearview mirror. "It's a party, not detention!"

I managed a weak smile, but that's about all I could do. After Jeff stopped the car in the driveway, Mom put a hand on his arm.

"They're going to love you," she said, and Jeff smiled at her.

Oh boy, is this how it's going to be? I wondered. But I still had another worry: Callie.

After we unloaded the car, we walked through the opened white gate into Callie's backyard, where the air already smelled like grilled hamburgers. Some of Callie's aunts and uncles were milling around, and Callie and her mom were

56

standing by the gate, anxiously waiting to meet Jeff. When Callie saw him, her whole face was a big "oh" of surprise and shock. I wonder if that's how I looked when I first saw Mr. Green in my kitchen.

"Mr. Green!" Callie blurted out. Then she hastily added, "I already did my math homework from the extra-help class!"

Jeff laughed. "Don't worry, I promise I'm not here to talk about math," he said. Then he turned to Mrs. Wilson and shook her hand. "Barbara, it's so nice to meet you. Happy birthday!"

"It's my pleasure," she replied. "Sharon has told us so much about you."

I could see Callie's blue eyes practically burning through me with curiosity, so I walked up to her dad, who was working the grill.

"Hey, Mr. Wilson," I said. "I brought the vanilla cupcakes. And I made taco dip. It's extra spicy."

Callie's dad put down his barbecue tongs and gave me a big hug. "That's my girl. Look at you, Katie! You're growing like a weed!"

It was a good hug. I've known Callie's dad since I was a baby, and he's probably the closest thing I have to a real dad. Only I don't see him so much anymore since Callie and I aren't friends.

"I only grew an inch over the last few months," I reported. (I measure myself every week against the doorjamb in my room. I don't care about being tall—I'm just curious.)

"Well, that's some inch, then," Mr. Wilson said. "Are you sure you're not wearing high heels?"

I laughed and looked down at my sneakers, which were covered with rainbows I had drawn on with some Magic Marker. "Me? Heels? No way."

"You should see the heels that Callie just bought," Mr. Wilson said. "I don't see how she can walk in them, honestly."

Callie walked up and grabbed me by the arm. "I'll show them to her, and she can be the judge," she said. But I knew why she was really dragging me up to her room.

"Why didn't you tell me about Mr. Green?" she asked after slamming the door shut behind her.

I just looked at her. I don't tell Callie anything anymore, so why would I tell her about Mr. Green?

But Callie didn't even wait for a response. "I mean, it's weird your mom is dating anybody, right? And it's a teacher on top of that? Seriously, how are you okay with that?"

Callie sounded genuinely sympathetic, and suddenly it was like we had never stopped being friends.

I mean, we had spent almost every day together practically since the day I was born. (Callie is three months older.) She used to know every detail of my life—every hope and every secret.

I sighed and sat down on Callie's bed. "I'm not sure if I'm okay with the whole thing," I confessed. "I mean, it's weird. And Mom told Jeff about me before I knew he was Mr. Green."

"Jeff? You get to call him Jeff?" Callie asked.

"Only when we're out of school," I answered. "See what I mean? Weird!"

"So I guess your mom really likes him, then," Callie said. "I don't think she would put you through this if she didn't."

"I know, and that's good, but it's also bad," I said. "If she likes him that much, they might get married. And I might have to move. Or share my room with his daughter."

"Did she say she was going to marry him?" Callie asked.

I shook my head.

"Then don't stress just yet," Callie said. "Your mom waited this long to get a boyfriend. She's probably not going to jump into marrying somebody right away."

"True," I admitted.

"And I bet your mom wouldn't make you move if you didn't want to," Callie said. "She loves you, Katie. You're, like, her whole world."

"I *was* her whole world," I corrected her. "Now Jeff is part of that world. And, lately, it feels like he's the Pacific Ocean or something and I'm just a tiny little island."

"That's not true. You're still the most important thing in her life," Callie said convincingly. "And at least Mr. Green is supernice. And cute!"

I rolled my eyes as Callie giggled. "Yeah, because I care about a cute stepdad," I said. And then I started giggling too.

That's when Mom knocked on the door. "Girls, the food is ready," she said, and then she saw us both laughing. "Well, that's a nice sight to see."

I had to agree. It was nice to laugh with Callie again.

Mom went back downstairs, and I got up from the bed.

"I haven't told anyone else about Mr. Green," I said, knowing Callie would understand.

Callie nodded. "Come on, let's get a burger before my dad eats them all."

And, suddenly, things weren't weird anymore, just like that. Because when it came right down to it, Jeff was really nice. Mom was really happy. And Callie and I were good.

Maybe things are going to be okay, I thought. *Maybe I was thinking about this all wrong. I immediately assumed the worst when I found out my mom was dating Mr. Green, but what if it turned out to be just the opposite? Maybe things would just keep getting better and better. Only time will tell.*

CHAPTER 9

The Secret Is Out

The rest of the day was pretty fun. We all played volleyball together, and I found out Jeff is just as bad as I am at playing volleyball. (In fact, I'm so bad that George calls me "Silly Arms" after that sprinkler with a bunch of arms that wave and wiggle all over the place. I guess that's what I look like when I play.)

When Jeff dropped us off at home, Mom and I showered and got into our pj's and ate leftover taco dip while we watched the food channel. So it was cool we could have Jeff time and then Mom and Katie time all in the same day.

That's why I was in a pretty good mood at school the next day—until lunch, anyway. I was eating a sandwich and cracking up with Mia,

Alexis, and Emma about something that happened in gym class when Olivia Allen marched up to our table.

Olivia has thick brown hair, with brown bangs across her forehead. She gets pretty dressed up for school, and today she was wearing black tights with a black denim skirt and a shimmery silver top. She stood there, posed with her hands on her hips, like a model in a magazine. I figured she was going to ask Mia something, or say something dumb about my purple jeans, but I wasn't prepared for what she actually said.

"I can't believe your mom is dating Mr. Green!"

My stomach sank. I could see Mia and Alexis practically choking on their sandwiches, and Emma's eyes were huge. I knew they were probably mad I didn't tell them, but I had to deal with Olivia first.

"So?" I asked, trying to look like I didn't care.

Olivia stood there, not knowing what to say. I guess she was hoping for more details, but I wasn't about to give them up.

Olivia's brain must have gotten tired, because she just tossed her hair behind her shoulder and walked away—back to the table where she sat with Callie and the other girls in the BFC. I was so mad at Callie! After everything we had talked about yesterday, she had gone and blabbed to the BFC. How could she?

I turned back to the table, and my friends were all staring at me.

"How come you didn't tell us?" Mia asked. She didn't sound angry, thankfully—just surprised and a little bit hurt.

"I'm sorry!" I blurted out. "It was just . . . so weird! I didn't want anyone to know."

"So it's true?" Alexis asked.

I nodded. "Yes. Jeff is Mr. Green. I didn't know either until I met him that night."

"Can you help me with my math homework?" Emma asked, and everyone giggled. That's when I knew that everything was okay.

"It is definitely weird," Mia said. "Super extra weird. I didn't think parents were even allowed to date teachers."

"We can check the school handbook, but I'm sure it's allowed," Alexis said. "At least, maybe it is as long as Mr. Green isn't teaching Katie."

"Yeah, Mom said that might be an issue. So I guess it's good I have Mr. K. for math," I said.

Then Mia let out a little squeal. "Wait a second. So Mr. Green was actually in your house?"

"Yeah, he ate dinner with us, and then we watched a movie," I replied.

"Is he the same out of school as he is when he's in school?" Emma asked, her blue eyes filled with curiosity.

"Yes," I answered. "He's nice, and he's funny."

"I still can't believe it," Mia said, shaking her head. "Your mom's boyfriend is Mr. Green. Weird!"

Alexis's eyes suddenly narrowed. "Wait a second. How does Callie know?"

I sighed. "Yesterday. Mom invited Jeff to go with us to Callie's mom's birthday party. I told Callie not to tell anybody," I said, but as soon as the words came out, I realized I might not have said that, exactly. I told Callie nobody else knew. But she should have understood!

Alexis made a face. "If the BFC knows, then the whole school will know soon."

"That's what I'm worried about."

"Nobody will care," Emma tried to reassure me, but I wasn't so sure.

As I finished my sandwich, I looked over at Callie. I was hoping she'd look over at me, so I could give her my mad face. But she and Olivia were talking and laughing and not looking in my direction.

I opened up my lunch bag and took out a cupcake. It was a vanilla one from the batch we made for Callie's party, only I had put lots of sprinkles on this one. (I am a little sprinkle crazy these days.)

As I took a bite, I heard a voice behind me.

"Hey, the sprinkler is eating sprinkles!"

It was George. I don't mind him teasing me, because I know he's just trying to make me laugh.

"Cool! Did you bring one for me?" George asked.

I laughed. "Sorry," I said. "Next time, I promise."

"Well, as long as you promise," George said, and then he walked back to his table.

"He *so* likes you," Alexis said.

"I know," I said, smiling.

Mia suddenly started cracking up.

"What?" I asked.

"I just had the funniest thought, but it's bad," she said, still giggling.

"Come on, tell me," I urged.

She caught her breath. "You and George could double-date with your mom and Mr. Green."

"No way!" I playfully punched her in the arm, and I laughed with her.

I was glad my friends understood the Mr. Green

thing. Now I just had to worry about Callie—and what the rest of the school would think. When the lunch bell rang, I quickly caught up to Callie.

"Hey," I said, tapping her on the shoulder.

Callie turned, smiling. "Oh, hey, Katie."

"Please don't tell anyone else about Mr. Green," I said, and Callie's smile faded. "That was between you and me, okay?"

Callie looked stunned, and I didn't wait for her to answer. I just turned and kept walking down the hall. I didn't know if Callie would listen, but at least I had talked to her.

CHAPTER 10

A Surprise Guest

On Wednesday we had another Cupcake Club meeting at my house. Wednesday was turning out to be a good day for everyone to meet, because it didn't interfere with Mia and Alexis playing soccer or Emma's flute practice. Everyone came over after school, and Alexis got right down to business.

"Mrs. Martinez e-mailed me, and she says they just want vanilla and chocolate cupcakes for the event, because she says most kids like those," she reported. "For the vanilla cupcakes, we can make angel food, because we already have all the ingredients. But we can decorate them any way we want."

"I have some ideas," Mia said, opening up her sketchbook. "The first one is fun. It's an alien.

See? We frost the cupcake with green frosting, use black icing gel to draw a mouth, and those eyes are those round white mints with black gel for the pupils."

"Are those candy antennae?" I asked, looking at the picture she had drawn. "They're so cute!"

"And then these are more space themed," Mia said, turning the page. The picture showed a cupcake with blue icing and yellow stars. "We can cut out the stars from fruit strips."

"These look great," Alexis said, and Emma nodded.

"But will we be able to do them without you?" I asked a little nervously.

"Of course!" Mia said. "They're easy. The alien mouths are basically circles. And I can cut out stars in advance. Eddie says he'll help me make the display, too. Check it out."

Mia showed us another sketch. The display was a cone-shape rocket ship with rings going around it that were wide enough to hold the cupcakes.

"That is awesome!" I said.

"We're going to paint the rocket ship silver, and the rings will be dark blue, with planets and stars, so it looks like the rocket is flying through space," Mia explained.

"It's perfect," Alexis said. "And we can get a dark-blue paper tablecloth for the table."

"And dark-blue little plates and napkins," Emma added.

Alexis started typing on her laptop. "Perfect!" she said. Then she looked up, pushing a strand of her curly red hair behind her ear. "So, let's get to making those angel food cupcakes."

"Why are we making these again?" I asked. "They need a whole dozen egg whites, and Mom and I never know what to do with the extra yolks."

I don't know if you've ever had angel food cake, but it's made with lots of whipped-up egg whites and no yolks. The cake is perfectly white and also very light and fluffy.

"We've been getting a lot of requests for lighter cupcakes," Alexis explained. "I guess people want to be able to eat a cupcake without a lot of guilt. I've made a chart to show the increase in demand, if you want to see it."

Nobody argued with Alexis. When she suggests something, she usually has a million facts to back it up. Plus, it was actually a pretty good idea.

"Let's do white chocolate frosting," Emma said. "White chocolate is one of our most-requested flavors. And we can dye the frosting blue, for the space themed cupcakes. Those can be the angel food cupcakes."

I nodded. "Sounds good. I'll start separating the eggs."

Separating eggs takes a steady hand. You have to carefully crack the egg and then gently tip both halves of the shell so that the white pours into the bowl while the yolk stays in the shell. Then you put the yolk into a separate bowl. You have to make sure the yolk doesn't break, because even if you get a little bit of yolk in the white, it won't whip up very well.

Mia helped me with the eggs, and soon they were whipping up nicely in the stand mixer. Alexis was melting white chocolate chips in the microwave for the icing, and Emma was measuring the dry ingredients for the cupcakes.

"So, did Olivia say anything more about Mr. Green?" Mia asked me.

I shook my head. "No, and so far it hasn't been a huge deal. I'm not sure why Olivia isn't blabbing it all over the school." It occurred to me that maybe Callie had talked to her, but I wasn't counting on it. "Maybe she just doesn't want me to get attention for it. You know how she is. She likes the spotlight for herself."

"Believe me, I know," Mia said as she slowly added the dry ingredients to the mixer.

Soon the cupcakes were in the oven, and we continued with our usual routine. We snacked on peanut butter and apples while the cupcakes baked and cooled, and then we started frosting them.

"They smell great," Emma remarked, holding up an iced cupcake. "And they look pretty nice. Boring but nice."

"I think they need some flair," I said, and I went to the pantry to get some rainbow sprinkles. When I came back, I started showering the cupcakes.

Mia was laughing. "Katie! You can't put rainbows on everything!"

"Why not?" I asked.

We were all laughing when the doorbell rang, and I heard my mom answer it. Then my friends got strangely quiet, and I looked up from the cupcakes to see Mr. Green standing in the kitchen doorway.

"Hi, girls," he said, with a little wave.

"Oh hi, Je—Mr. Green," I said. It felt too weird to call him Jeff in front of my friends, even though he was in my house.

Mom stepped into the kitchen. "Jeff just stopped by to pick up a book I'm lending him," she said.

"And then I smelled the cupcakes, so I couldn't resist seeing what you guys were up to," he said. "I hope you don't mind."

"It's fine!" Emma said superquickly. I could tell everyone felt a little awkward.

Mr. Green eyed the cupcakes on the kitchen table. "You know, if you ever need an official taster, I'm up for the job."

"You'd have to fight my brother Matt for that job," Emma said.

"Or my stepdad, Eddie!" Mia added, and we all laughed. But the word "stepdad" got kind of stuck in my head. Would Jeff be my stepdad one day? Maybe it wouldn't be so bad. He was just as nice as Eddie, and Mia liked Eddie a lot.

Alexis put a cupcake on a plate and handed it to him. "But those other testers aren't here tonight, so you can have the job for now," she said. "It's an angel food cupcake. We're experimenting with a lighter cupcake recipe."

"Good idea," Mr. Green said. He took a seat at the kitchen table. Then he picked up the cupcake and stared at it very solemnly. He waved it in front of his nose. "Chocolate, with a hint of sprinkles. Interesting."

We all started giggling, because Mr. Green was

pretty funny. He carefully took a bite of the cupcake. Then he nodded his head, like he was thinking. Then he took another bite, and another, until there were nothing but crumbs left on the plate.

"Delicious," he said. "The cake is light and fluffy and perfect. The sprinkles were a nice touch. And the frosting is tasty, but I wonder if it's a little too heavy for the light cupcake?"

I looked at Mia and raised an eyebrow. Most of our cupcake tasters give us a thumbs-up or thumbs-down. This was the first time we had gotten real criticism.

"What do you mean?" I asked.

He picked up another cupcake and broke it in half. "See how the weight of the icing crumbles the cake underneath?" he asked. "You might want to try to make something a little lighter, like a lemon frosting, maybe. You could make it with skim milk, so it wouldn't be thick—more like a glaze. But it would be another way to lighten up the cake."

My fellow Cupcake Club members and I were all a little bit stunned. Not only was Mr. Green nice and funny . . . but he could bake? It was kind of hard to believe.

Mom walked to the refrigerator. "I've got lemons and skim milk, if you want to try a batch."

I looked at Mr. Green. "Can you show us?"

He nodded. "Sure thing."

We washed out the bowl of the stand mixer, and then Mr. Green nodded to Alexis.

"We need two cups of powdered sugar," he said.

"We shouldn't make a big batch," Alexis said. (She doesn't like wasting supplies, which is smart.) "We only have half of the cupcakes left to frost."

"Ah, a teachable moment," Mr. Green said, lighting up. "Now we can halve the recipe."

We all groaned, but we were laughing too, because we knew Mr. Green was mostly kidding.

"This is way too easy," I said. "Half of two cups is one cup."

"That is an A-plus answer," Mr. Green said, smiling, and then he showed us how to mix the sugar with skim milk, lemon juice, and a little vanilla. When it was done, he stuck a spoon in it and held it out to me. "What do you think?"

I tasted it. "Lemony and tangy, but still sweet," I said. "Delicious."

The rest of the Cupcake Club tried it and agreed. Then we applied the glaze to the cupcakes, which was tricky because it was kind of loose and drippy. But it looked nice and shiny when it was on.

"They're pretty but plain," Mia remarked. "They

need something else—and not rainbow sprinkles this time, Katie."

"Fine. I have all kinds of sprinkles!" I said, running to the pantry. I came back with white edible glitter and sprinkled it on top. "Perfect!"

Mia studied the result. "Not bad. But I bet pale-yellow glitter would look even better."

"We should hire you as a consultant," Alexis said to Mr. Green.

He laughed. "That's flattering, but I will gladly volunteer my help whenever you need it."

"So how did you learn how to bake, anyway?" Alexis asked.

"Probably like you did," he replied. "I like to eat, so I started reading recipes. And my daughter has a sweet tooth, so I've had a lot of opportunities to try out new recipes on her."

Then he rolled up his sleeves. "Let me help you guys clean this up."

"That's the girls' job," my mom said. "Come on; let me get you that book."

They left us in the kitchen, and we started to clean up.

"I don't know if it's possible, but I think Mr. Green is even cooler than he was before," Alexis said.

Emma nodded. "Definitely."

Mia looked at me. "I know it's still weird that he's dating your mom, but at the same time it's kind of cool, isn't it?"

"Yeah, I think so," I agreed. "I just need some time to get used to it."

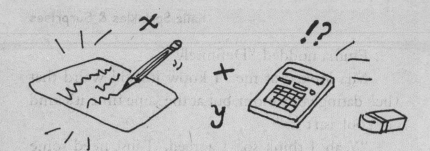

CHAPTER 11

Some Extra Help

It was almost six o'clock when the Cupcake Club meeting ended, and my friends all left, waving good-bye to Mr. Green. I noticed he was sticking around a lot longer than somebody who'd just come to pick up a book.

"I asked Jeff to stay for dinner," Mom told me when I was done saying good-bye to everyone. "There's plenty of soup in the Crock-Pot, and I can make some grilled cheese sandwiches to go with it."

"Okay," I said, and I realized I didn't mind. It was actually kind of nice that Mr. Green—I mean, Jeff—was staying.

I set the table while Mom made the grilled cheese, and I noticed she was making her fancy grilled cheese, with sliced pears and Gruyere cheese on multigrain bread, instead of plain old American cheese on white. It didn't take long before we were all sitting around the dinner table. It was kind of fun having a new person to sit and eat with us. It's almost always just me and Mom, and we usually run out of things to say to each other. But Jeff has all these funny stories that he tells.

Like this one about when he was eleven years old: "So I made these wings out of an old rain poncho and some wood, and I actually thought I could fly if the wind was right," he told us. "So I waited for a windy day, and then I climbed on top of the garage."

Mom was laughing really hard. "Oh no! I can just picture you up there."

"What happened?" I asked.

"Well, they didn't work, of course," Jeff said. "But luckily my dad had just had a load of mulch delivered, so it broke my fall. I was pretty smelly, but I didn't get hurt."

"Did your dad get mad?" I asked.

"A little," Jeff replied. "But I'm lucky. He always encouraged me to explore the things I was curious about."

"I guess Mom does that with me, too."

Jeff looked at Mom and smiled, and I sensed another gooey moment was coming, so I quickly got up.

"I'd better go do my homework," I said.

"What do you have tonight?" Mom asked.

"A Spanish worksheet, a paragraph for English, and I have to study for a math test," I reported, making a face.

Jeff noticed. "Uh-oh. You're not digging the math?"

"It has never been my best subject," I admitted. "I get confused by some of the algebra stuff, and, well . . . Mr. K. sometimes explains stuff really fast, and I can't keep up."

"Do you want some help?" Jeff asked.

I was a little surprised. "Wouldn't that be cheating?"

Jeff laughed. "I didn't say I'd take the test for you. I said I'd help and answer any questions you have, just like I'd do for any student in after-school help."

Mom looked so relieved. "Oh, we'd be grateful!" she said. "I can only help her so much."

She looked at me expectantly, but I pretty much thought it was cool that Jeff wanted to help me, so I didn't object. I went and got my math binder, and when I came back, the kitchen table was cleared off and Mom had put on a pot of coffee for her and Jeff.

"It's all the equations," I said, opening up to my study notes. "I never know where to start."

"That can be confusing," Jeff said. "But I can give you some simple tips, so you can figure it out. Let's start with this first problem here."

I won't bore you with my algebra, but basically what happened was that Jeff explained things really clearly—and slowly. Maybe I just needed some one-on-one time with a teacher. Because after an hour of studying with Jeff, I felt like I finally understood.

"Wow, thank you," I said when we were done. "You're a great tutor."

"Thanks," Jeff said. "I get a lot of practice with my daughter."

"You mean Emily?" I asked.

Jeff nodded. "I have some pictures, if you want to see."

"Sure," I said.

Jeff took out his phone and started scrolling through his pictures. "Here're some recent ones."

The first one showed Emily, with a crown on, at her birthday party, and she was blowing out the candles on a cake. She had brown hair and kind of looked like Jeff, but I noticed she had brown eyes, like me. That led me to an interesting thought. Let's just say Emily and I became stepsisters someday. We looked similar enough that people might think we were actually sisters. There was something about that that felt nice.

The rest of the pictures showed Emily in her soccer uniform and Emily making a sand castle on the beach. She was smiling in every picture.

"She looks nice," I remarked.

"She is," Jeff said. "I think you girls would like each other."

I nodded, thinking. If Emily and I did meet, that might mean that Mom and Jeff were really serious. I was slowly getting used to that idea, and it wasn't so bad.

CHAPTER 12

Back and Forth

Okay, class, who's ready for a math test?"

"Me!" I called out cheerfully. Most of the other kids in class, including Mia, just groaned. But I felt pretty excited. As soon as Jared Fogelson, who sat in the seat of front of me, handed back the test sheet, I got started.

I looked at the first problem, and I knew what to do! I took my time, just like Jeff had suggested, and when I finished with all the answers, I went back and checked the hard ones. Even after all that I was still one of the first ones done.

Mr. K. was checking his e-mail when I got to his desk.

"That's fast for you, Katie. Did you check your work?" he asked.

"Yup," I said.

"Awesome!" said Mr. K. with a smile.

I went back to my desk, feeling really good. To pass the time until class ended, I took out my notebook and started drawing rainbows and shooting stars.

When I sailed into the lunchroom later that day, I was in a great mood. And as soon as the whole Cupcake Club was seated together, we started talking about Mr. Green.

"I can't believe how nice he is in person!" Emma said.

Alexis giggled. "Emma, you see him in person every day in math class."

Emma blushed a little. "You know what I mean. What other math teacher has ever made icing with us before?"

Then Mia nodded her head to the side, and we realized Mr. Green was heading our way.

"Hi, Je—Mr. Green," I said, stopping myself from calling him by his first name.

"Hi, girls," he said pleasantly. "Katie, how did you do on your math test?"

"I think I aced it!" I reported.

"Great work!" Mr. Green said, and then he winked and moved on to the next table.

"That was weird," Alexis said after he walked away. "He acted like we didn't all hang out together yesterday."

"Maybe he's trying to keep the Mr. Green at school separate from the Mr. Green at home," Mia reasoned.

I thought about this. That made sense, but I didn't like it very much. "So that means every time I see Mr. Green in school, I have to pretend he's not dating my mom? And eating at my house? And helping us make cupcakes?"

Alexis nodded sympathetically. "It's like you've got to turn a switch on and off all the time. That kind of stinks."

I sighed. "Well, at least I think I did okay on my test."

We dug in to our food, and I noticed Mia was picking at her salad. It occurred to me that she had been quiet on the bus this morning too.

"Are you okay?" I asked.

"I guess," she said. She put down her fork. "Last night I got into this fight with Eddie. Mom was out and I was home with Eddie, and he asked me to empty the dishwasher. But I said it was Dan's turn, and then Eddie said no, it wasn't. And I couldn't believe he didn't believe me. It was so unfair."

"Did he yell at you?" Emma asked.

Mia shook her head. "No, but he said annoying stuff, like, 'I expect a better attitude from you, Mia.' I already have to hear that from Mom and Dad. And now there's a third person saying it too? It's too much!"

I let this sink in. Mia almost never complained about Eddie. I guess it was normal they wouldn't get along all the time. But then I thought, what if Mr. Green was, like, telling me to clean my room one minute, and then I'd have to see him in school the next day? That would be so not cool.

Yesterday had been fun and shiny and happy, but now I was starting to have different thoughts. I liked that Mom was dating Jeff. But I didn't like that she was dating Mr. Green.

When Mom got home from work later that day, I asked her, "So, does Jeff need to borrow any more books?"

Mom gave me a kind of funny look, and then she said, "No, Katie, it's just you and me tonight."

"Cool," I said, trying not to sound too excited or anything, but honestly I was relieved it was just going to be me and Mom. "So what's for dinner?"

"I thought we could do Pajama Dinner," Mom answered.

"Yes!" I yelled. That's one of my favorite things. Mom and I put on our pajamas early and eat breakfast for dinner. Yes, it's dorky, but the breakfast almost always includes bacon, and bacon is basically the best food ever. And everything is better when you wear your pajamas. I think everyone should try a Pajama Dinner at least once.

"What's your homework situation?" Mom asked.

"Finished it," I told her. "I only had social studies and Spanish tonight."

"Good," Mom said. "Time for pj's!"

I ran upstairs to get on my pajamas. It helped that a rainstorm had started to whip up outside, so it was already dark, and a little chilly—perfect pajama weather.

Mom and I cooked together. She fried up some bacon, and I made French toast with cinnamon and vanilla, and we also took some leftover potatoes and made hash browns. Yum!

We could hear the rain dancing on the roof as we ate our delicious food in our cozy kitchen, and Mom and I talked about school and her favorite patient, Mrs. Greenberg, who just turned ninety, and a whole bunch of stuff—except for Jeff. After we cleaned up we watched some TV, and I snuggled up on the couch next to Mom and sighed.

It was a perfect night. And then I thought, what if Jeff was here all the time? Would Mom and I still do Pajama Dinners? That would be weird.

I was starting to feel like there was a tennis match going on in my head. Last night it felt good having Jeff around. Today it felt really good *not* having him around. It was so confusing!

I tried to push those confusing feelings away. Right now, on the couch with Mom, everything felt perfect.

"I wish things could be like this forever," I said sleepily. Mom squeezed me a little and gently pushed a strand of hair away from my face, but she didn't say anything.

CHAPTER 13

Leave It to Olivia . . .

The next morning I got on to the bus and sat next to Mia, like I always do. Emma and Alexis live close to the school, so they walk every morning. I'm really glad Mia takes the bus with me, because we can talk and talk for the whole ride.

That morning I had something on my mind.

"So are you still mad at Eddie?" I asked.

Mia shrugged. "No. I was just in a bad mood yesterday, I guess. He's mostly okay. It just stinks sometimes when your parents are divorced, you know? It's hard to figure out everything."

I nodded. I wasn't in Mia's situation, but I knew how complicated things could get. My own dad suddenly reappeared in my life a little while ago, sending me an e-mail saying that he wanted to see me again. He has this whole new family with three daughters and everything. I told him I wasn't ready to see him yet, and I'm still not sure if I'm ready.

So the whole time I'd been worrying about Jeff becoming my stepdad and what it would be like to have a stepsister, I've had this whole other situation that was always in the back of my mind. It was a lot to worry about, and it was kind of all happening at once. But at least I had a friend like Mia who understood what I was going through.

George stuck his head over the back of our seat. "Hey, Katie," he said.

"Hey, George," I replied.

"So Mrs. Kratzer said we have to pick partners for the social studies project today," he said. "Want to be mine?"

Next to me, Mia had this big grin on her face. I tried not to blush.

"Well, Mia is usually my partner," I said.

"That's okay," Mia said quickly. "I already partnered with someone else."

"You did?" I asked, surprised.

Mia gave me a look telling me to just go with it. "Yeah, remember? So you can partner with George."

"Oh, right," I said, and now I was definitely blushing. "Sure, I'll do it."

George smiled. "Cool! I have some ideas already."

Then he disappeared back behind the seat, and Mia turned to me, still grinning.

"Why did you do that?" I hissed.

"Because he so likes you, and you like him," she whispered. "Why doesn't he just ask you out again already? I mean, after you went to the pep-rally parade together, I thought you'd be, like, going out."

"The pep-rally parade wasn't a big deal," I answered. "Anyway, it doesn't matter because Mom says I can't date until I'm a junior in high school."

"But that's practically forever!" Mia looked horrified.

"It's not so bad," I told her. "My life is complicated enough without having a boyfriend to worry about."

"Definitely," Mia agreed. "Still, you guys make a cute couple."

I nudged her. "Don't let him hear you!" And then we were both giggling again.

The bus pulled up in front of the school. It may have rained the night before, but the morning was beautiful, with fluffy white clouds in the bright blue sky. It was the kind of day that just makes you feel happy, you know?

So my morning got off to a good start, and it got even better when math class started, believe it or not. Mr. K. started off by passing out the graded math tests.

"Nice effort on this test, class," he said. I anxiously waited for him to hand mine to me. I was sure I had done pretty well. Seeing a B on the top of the paper would have made my day.

"Here you are, Katie," Mr. K. said, handing the paper to me. I couldn't believe the grade on top: 94. I got an A! An A on a math test! I don't think that has happened since I mastered the multiplication tables in third grade.

I almost jumped out of my seat and did a happy dance. Mia looked over at me, and I held up my paper.

I got an A! I mouthed, and then I saw Callie looking at me. If anybody would understand how much this A in math meant to me, it was Callie. She smiled at me and I smiled back. It's hard for me to stay really mad at her, you know?

I was still feeling superawesome about my A at lunchtime. When Mia, Alexis, and Emma were all seated, I produced the test and put it on the table with a flourish.

"Check it out," I said. "I got an A on my math test!"

My friends all cheered for me.

"I should have gone for extra help too," Mia said. "I studied, but I only got a B."

"You definitely need to go," I said. "Mr. Green is great. He really explains things well."

"So *that's* how you got an A!"

I turned around to see Olivia standing there with her hands on her hips. She must have been listening the whole time.

"You cheated!" she bellowed, loud enough for half the cafeteria to hear her. "Just because your mom is dating Mr. Green, he helps you get good math grades. I should have known!"

Olivia stormed back to the BFC table. I saw some girls at the next table whispering and then pointing over to me, thanks to Olivia and her loud mouth.

"I didn't cheat!" I fumed, and I didn't care who heard it. "Mr. Green just helped me study. He helps lots of kids."

"Of course you didn't cheat," Mia said soothingly.

"That is ridiculous!" Emma added.

Alexis looked angry. "She's just jealous. Don't listen to her."

"It doesn't matter if I listen to her or not," I said. "What if other kids listen to her?"

"Everyone knows Olivia is a big gossip," Alexis said, "and half the stuff she says isn't true. Nobody listens to her."

My friends made me feel better, like they always do. But I no longer felt like doing a happy dance, not even on this blue-skied, fluffy-clouded A day.

Why did Olivia have to spoil everything?

CHAPTER 14

Mom Did What?

After lunch I had social studies with Mrs. Kratzer. She has short hair and glasses and is just one of those people who looks like they love history, you know? She's pretty mellow, but when she tells us stories about stuff that happened in the past, she gets excited, doing voices and everything.

"Okay, class," she said in her regular mellow voice. "I'd like you to team up with your partner for the project."

George carried his chair over to my desk.

"Thanks for being my partner," George said.

"Thanks for asking me," I said, and then I cringed a little inside. That sounded really corny.

"Everyone, please get out your project sheets," instructed Mrs. Kratzer. "By Monday, I'd like each group to submit a description of your project."

The project sheet had a lot of suggestions on it. We were studying western expansion—you know, the explorers and pioneers who went out West in the 1800s. We had to pick a subject for our project plus the type of project we were supposed to do.

"It's Friday," I said. "How are we supposed to finish this by Monday?"

"Mom said you could come over tomorrow to work on it if you want," George said quickly, as if he had known this would come up.

I was a little surprised. I hadn't been to George's house since he invited his whole class to his dinosaur-themed birthday party in second grade.

"Um, okay. We don't have any cupcake jobs tomorrow," I said. "I should be able to come."

"I'm in your phone, right?" George asked quickly. He looked a little worried. I smiled and nodded. "Then text me when you talk to your mom."

"Okay," I agreed. "So, anyway, we should check out this list."

We were quiet for a while as we both looked at the list together. Then we both spoke up at the same time.

"I like Calamity Jane," I said.

"Calamity Jane sounds interesting," said George.

We burst out laughing, because it was so weird that we had the exact thought at the exact same time.

Thanks to George, I was on my way to being in a better mood again. Then as soon as class was over, Sophie and Lucy came up to me.

"Is it true that your mom is dating Mr. Green?" Sophie asked.

"Well, yeah," I said. There was no point in denying it, not after Olivia's outburst. "But it's not serious or anything." (Okay, that was kind of a lie, but if I wasn't ready for the truth yet, I didn't think the population of Park Street Middle School would be either.)

Lucy got a dreamy look in her eyes. "She's so lucky. He's so cute!"

"Yeah, people seem to think so," I said, suddenly feeling awkward again. "Okay, gotta get to class!"

I was pretty glad when the day was over. Mom wasn't there yet when I got home from school, so I did my homework until I heard her car in the driveway. I greeted her at the door with my A math paper in front of my face.

"Ta-da!" I announced.

"Oh, Katie, good for you!" Mom said, and I

lowered the paper, so I could see her face. "I'm so proud of you!"

"Thanks," I said. "Can you believe it? I got a ninety-four!"

Mom hugged me. "You have to tell Jeff!" she said. "He'll be so excited!"

Why in the world would Jeff be excited? I wondered. It was like Mom wanted Jeff to be part of everything we did. Although he did help me study, so maybe that's why.

Mom was already dialing his number. I could hear it ring a few times on the other side, and then Mom frowned a little. "Oh, that's right, he's out to dinner with Emily tonight."

That made sense. "You mean like how Mia goes to see her dad every other weekend?"

Mom nodded. "Jeff sees her just about every other weekend, and also one night a week, since he and Emily's mom live in the same town," she explained.

I was starting to get more and more curious about Emily. "I wonder what she's like," I mused, following Mom into her office as she dropped her briefcase on her desk.

"Oh, you'll love her when you meet her," Mom said, looking at me. "She's a lot like you."

I frowned. "How do you know?"

"Well, I've met her," Mom replied.

I let this sink in for a second. "You've met her?" I couldn't quite believe it.

"Well, yes," Mom said as if it was no big deal. "She's such a lovely girl, so polite, and she likes to run just like we all do, and she was telling us about how she wants to try out for the cross-country team in middle school, and——"

"YOU MET HER WITHOUT ME? AND YOU DIDN'T TELL ME?" I screamed.

I was having a major freak-out. First, Mom told Jeff about me, but I didn't know about him. And second, now she's met Emily? It's hard to explain why I felt so angry, but to me it felt like Mom was keeping secrets from me. That I wasn't part of this big new thing in her life. And that hurt.

"Katie, lower your voice," Mom said.

I ignored her. "WHAT ELSE ARE YOU HIDING FROM ME?" I shrieked.

Mom sighed, and her voice got firm. "Katie, I know there's a lot of new stuff here, and I know you are upset, but that's no excuse to yell. Please go to your room and calm down, and we'll talk about it when we've both had a chance to cool off."

I stormed up to my room, stomping hard on

each step on my way up. *What does Mom have to cool off about?* I fumed. *She's the one who's messing things up, not me.*

I slammed the door behind me and flopped onto my bed. I didn't feel like texting Mia or even putting on my headphones and listening to music. I just lay there like a log, staring at the tiny little flowers on my bedspread.

I guess I'm really good at doing nothing, because when Mom finally knocked on my door, I looked at my clock and saw that a half hour had passed. I didn't say "Come in," but Mom came in anyway.

"Can we talk now?" Mom asked.

I nodded, but I still didn't say anything.

"Okay," Mom began, sitting on the edge of my bed, "I know you think I 'hid' Jeff from you. But we just wanted to wait until the time was right, honestly. And then I met Emily, and then Jeff met you. We thought that was the best way to do it. There is no instruction book for this kind of thing, Katie. Jeff and I are trying to do our best to make this easy for everyone, but there are going to be some bumps along the road."

"Big bumps," I said. "Potholes. Craters. Giant valleys . . ."

Mom smiled a tiny bit, and I almost smiled

myself. I knew I was being kind of silly.

"Jeff and I were planning on doing something with both you and Emily very soon," Mom said. "I know there are a lot of changes here, Katie, but I need you to roll with me a bit and know that I have your best interest at heart. I'm trying to do the best that I can."

"But you don't see my side of it," I said. "You just get to go on fun dates and stuff and meet everybody, but I have to see Jeff at school and stuff, and it's weird."

Part of me wanted to tell her about Olivia's big scene today, but I held back.

"I get that," she said. "Okay, how about from now on, I promise to consider your side of things?"

"That would be good," I said.

"And maybe you can promise to trust me a little bit," Mom said. "And talk to me when you're upset. We don't need to yell at each other."

"Sorry," I said, looking down at my bedspread again.

Mom hugged me. "It's okay, sweetie," she said. "I love you so much. You will always be my number-one priority." (Which is just what Callie had said, remember? But it felt good to hear Mom say it.)

"Thank you," I said. Then I had an idea. "Hey, can we go out to dinner?"

"Well, I already defrosted some chicken . . . ," Mom said, but I could tell from her voice it was going to be easy to sway her.

"Come on. We need to celebrate my A," I reminded her.

Mom smiled. "Then the chicken can wait."

So Mom and I went out to eat at our favorite Indian restaurant, and I had honey ice cream for dessert, and I guess by the time the day was over, I was ready to do a happy dance again. Almost.

CHAPTER 15

Callie Steps Up

"Hey, Katie, come on in," George said.

I waved to Mom as she pulled away, and stepped into George's home, a brick house with white shutters on a perfectly mowed lawn. I could hear the sound of a radio blaring from somewhere inside the house, and George's twin brothers were running around the living room, screaming.

"Dad! Could you turn that off? Katie is here and we need to work," George yelled.

The radio went off, and George's dad stepped out of the kitchen, wiping his hands on a towel. "Sorry. Loud music helps me do the dishes," he said, and then he held out his hand. "Hello, Katie."

"Hi, Mr. Martinez," I said.

George nodded to me. "We can work in here."

I followed him to the dining room, where George had a laptop, notebook, pencils, and a plate of cookies set up on the table.

"I was going to make cupcakes, but I figured they wouldn't be as good as yours," he said.

I picked up a chocolate-chip cookie and bit into it. "That's okay. I love cookies! Did you really make these?"

"Dad helped," George admitted.

"They're really good," I said. "Thanks. So, um, let's get started."

I was kind of worried that it would be awkward to be in George's house, but we had so much to do that I didn't really have time to worry about that kind of stuff.

"So, Calamity Jane, right?" I began. "I was thinking that doing a skit might be fun. But the timeline would probably be easier."

"Let's go for the skit," George said. "It'll be more fun. And I bet we can make it funny."

"Definitely," I agreed. That's one thing I really like about George. He has a great sense of humor.

We figured it out, and then we did our list of props for the skit and decided who would get what. As George sent the file to the printer, his mom walked into the room.

"Why, hello, Katie," she said. "How's the project going?"

"I think it's going to be good," I replied.

"Alexis sent me some sketches of your cupcake designs," she said. "I'm very impressed. I know you girls are going to do a great job at the exhibit opening."

George came back in with our printed-out work. "Yeah, I told Mom how awesome you guys are."

"Thanks," I said. George and his mom were being so nice, but it only made me feel nervous. I was starting to feel really pressured about this cupcake job.

Then Mom came to pick me up.

"How did it go?" she asked, and she had a goofy smile on her face, like she was going to tease me about George or something.

"We got it done," I said, and I didn't give any more details.

Mia was with her dad that weekend, so the rest of the weekend was kind of boring. Mom and I went for a long run on Sunday, because the weather was cool and beautiful. We didn't talk about Jeff or Emily or even George at all, and that was kind of a relief.

❀

By the time Monday came around, I had pretty much forgotten about Olivia's outburst in the lunchroom. When I got off the bus, I was heading to my locker when Olivia approached me.

"Say, Katie, do you plan on cheating on your next math test again?" she asked loudly.

"Drop it, Olivia," I said. "I didn't cheat."

"That's what it looks like to me," said Olivia dramatically, raising her voice even more. "Since your mom and Mr. Green are dating, it makes sense he would give you all the answers in advance."

My face turned beet red. George, who had just walked past, stopped in his tracks.

"Your mom is dating Mr. Green?" George asked. He thought about it for a second, then smiled. "That's cool."

Leave it to George to be nice about it. But some of the other kids in the hallway were looking at me funny.

"Take it back, Olivia."

I turned around to see Callie standing behind me. She looked angry. "That's not true and you know it," Callie told Olivia.

"It *is* true!" Olivia protested. "You told me!"

"I said Katie's mom was dating Mr. Green, and

I shouldn't have told you that," Callie admitted. "That wasn't my news to tell. But I certainly did not tell you Katie was cheating. I've known Katie her whole life. She would never do that."

I was shocked. Was Callie really sticking up for me? Against Olivia Allen? I couldn't believe it, but I was really glad she was doing it.

Olivia wasn't about to admit defeat though. "Her timing was weird, don't you think?" she asked. "Katie isn't great at math, and then all of a sudden she gets an A, right after her mom starts dating Mr. Green?"

"First of all, Mr. Green doesn't even teach Mr. K.'s class, so how would he know the test answers in advance?" Callie pointed out. "And, anyway, Katie says she studied, and I believe her. Mr. Green runs the after-school help class. Anyone can go. You're just mad because you got a B minus on your test in Mr. Green's class. You could have gone for extra help too. But you didn't because the two of us went to the mall instead. You said you didn't need to study for your test."

"But I *had* to go to the mall. It's not my fault Mr. Green only gives extra help after school," Olivia said. "And I bet Mr. Green helps Katie right in her house! That's an unfair advantage."

I wasn't sure how Olivia guessed Mr. Green had helped me study at home, but she was right on target. And maybe she had a point. Was it unfair that Mr. Green helped me at home? I wasn't sure.

But Callie wasn't backing down either. "Isn't that why you're getting an A in Spanish?" she asked Olivia. "It's because your mom is a Spanish tutor! She studies with you whenever you want. It's the same thing."

Good point, Callie! I thought.

"It is not the same," Olivia protested, but I could tell she knew she was wrong.

Then the first bell rang, and everyone hurried off to homeroom. I was never more happy to hear that bell!

I didn't talk to Callie again until we had gym class together. I stopped her as she was going into the locker room.

"Thanks," I said, "for sticking up for me."

"I shouldn't have told Olivia about your mom," Callie said. "I'm sorry about that. I just thought it was so cool that Mr. Green was at my house, and I had to give people a reason why he was there. . . ."

"It's okay," I said. "I guess people are going to find out, anyway." *And once they do, what is the worst they could do?* I realized. Besides, I was never really one to worry about what other kids thought. Why start now?

And then I also remembered that George had said it was cool that Mom was dating Mr. Green. And Callie thought it was cool that he was at her house. And Sophie and Lucy had seemed excited the other day too. So maybe it wasn't embarrassing that Mom was dating Mr. Green. Maybe it was cool. Maybe some kids would even be jealous (but not in an angry Olivia way). I hadn't thought of that before.

"Well, keep me posted," Callie said, and then she headed into the locker room.

Like I said before, Callie and I stopped telling each other stuff since middle school started. But I still missed her, and what she did at my locker was really nice. I guess it couldn't hurt to keep her posted, could it? I mean, it was nice having Callie in my life once in a while. It's sort of like rainbow sprinkles. It's nice to have green and blue and red and yellow ones, but when you add pink or orange or purple, it's even better.

CHAPTER 16

Cupcakes from Outer Space

$\mathcal{M}$om and I were eating chicken and rice casserole that night, and I had just finished telling her that my Calamity Jane skit with George was a huge hit at school when she looked up at me and cleared her throat. She always does that before she has something she wants to discuss—like school or the importance of flossing my teeth every day or how I need to stop leaving my dirty clothes on the floor of my room. But I figured that this had something to do about Jeff, and I was right.

"So Jeff and I talked about it," Mom said. "And we decided that it's time for all of us to get together—you and me and Jeff and Emily."

"That's nice," I said casually, but inside I was pretty excited. Even after everything that happened, I was curious to meet Emily.

"We're going for pizza next Saturday night," Mom said. "Emily's mom is going out of town so Jeff will have her for the weekend. The sooner the better, we thought."

"Don't forget I have the children's museum thing," I reminded her.

Mom nodded. "I know. And Jeff and Emily are doing the charity run for the hospital. But we're meeting them at seven, and you'll all be done and cleaned up long before then."

I told my friends about it the next day at lunch (after I made sure Olivia wasn't eavesdropping nearby).

"So next Saturday, after the exhibit opening, I get to meet Emily," I said.

"You mean Mr. Green's daughter?" Emma asked. "That's so exciting!"

"I remember the first time I met Dan," Mia said. "Eddie made us all dinner, and Dan made this really loud burp at the end."

"Gross!" I cried. "Well, we're going out for pizza. But that's a good tip: Don't burp."

"And don't get pizza sauce on your face," Alexis advised.

"Or on your shirt," Emma added.

"Or you should wear a purple shirt in case you do spill your pizza sauce," Mia suggested. "You look great in purple, and it's dark enough to hide any sauce stains."

"Ahh! This is becoming complicated now!" I wailed.

"It's okay! We're just kidding," Mia said, patting my shoulder. "Just be regular awesome Katie and you'll be fine."

"But what if she's expecting *extra* awesome Katie?" I worried out loud.

Mia laughed. "You are hopeless!"

"Since you're going to see Mr. Green, maybe you could ask him for more ideas for lighter cupcakes," Alexis said. "When I told my mom about the angel food cupcakes, she flipped out. She said maybe her tennis club would order them for their big match. But we should probably have one or two more choices besides the angel food."

I nodded. "Sure, I bet he'll have some good ideas."

So, the rest of the week was pretty normal. I did see a few kids whispering when I came around, but nobody said anything bad about the Mr. Green thing. And a couple of people, like my friend Beth, came up to me and said stuff like, "It's so cool your mom is dating Mr. Green. What's he like?" And that was okay.

When the weekend rolled around, we only had a week to get ready for the big space exhibit at the children's museum. We met at Mia's house on Saturday afternoon. It was a nice day, so Eddie had set up stuff outside so we could finish the rocket ship display.

"Look what Eddie and I did," Mia said, holding up a piece of wood, cut to look like a rocket ship. "Eddie showed me how to use a jigsaw!"

"Oh my gosh! That is awesome," I said. "You can really cut all the curved lines like that?"

Mia grinned. "Yeah. But I had to go real slow."

"You're a natural with tools, Mia," Eddie said. "I always wanted to get Dan interested in woodworking, but he never got into it. Maybe you can be my new assistant. It's kind of like making clothes, only it's wood."

"That makes no sense!" Mia said, rolling her eyes, but you could tell she was teasing. I guess she wasn't mad at him anymore. That was good to know.

Then Mia pointed to a plastic tub that held all these little bottles of paint in every color you could think of. "We can paint the display, and when it's dry, Eddie will put it together for us."

"We need to practice the decorations, too," Alexis reminded her. "I brought a dozen vanilla cupcakes and some vanilla icing."

"Alexis, you think of everything!" I said.

Alexis grinned. "Yes, I do."

We painted the spaceship silver with red and blue accents, and then we painted the rings dark blue. Mia had drawn planets and stars using a computer program, and she printed out a bunch of them and cut them out.

"I'll glue those on at the end," she said.

"This is going to look so cool!" I said.

After we were done painting, we washed up and gathered in Mia's kitchen to practice the decorations. Alexis took notes while Mia dyed the icing in perfect shades of space blue and alien green. She showed us how to cut out stars from the fruit strips using the tiny cookie cutters she had bought. But the most fun was putting together the alien faces. Mia was right; drawing on the little mouth wasn't hard at all, and the white googly eyes and antennae looked really cute.

Eddie came in while we were decorating and held up one of the alien cupcakes in front of his face. "Take me to your leader," he said in an alien voice.

"That is so corny!" Mia complained.

Then I picked up one of the cupcakes with stars on it. I made it swoop through the air, like a spaceship.

"Presenting . . . cupcaaaaakes from spaaaace," I said in a deep movie-announcer voice.

"*You* are from space," Mia said, giggling.

"I can see Earth from up here," I said. "And I hear something too. It's Olivia Allen gossiping! I can hear her all the way from space!"

"Oh no!" Emma cried, laughing.

"So true," Alexis said.

Then I landed my space-traveling cupcake on the kitchen table. "Seriously, these cupcakes are perfect. I hope we can make them look this good next week."

"Of course we can," Alexis said. "I took notes on everything."

"It's easy," Mia said. "What could go wrong?"

"Do not say that!" I said. "You'll jinx us!"

Mia shook her head. "Stop worrying so much."

Mom tells me that too. But of course I worry. Because in my life it seems like if something can go wrong, it will!

CHAPTER 17

It Happened in Slow Motion. . . .

"Wow! These are looking really great," I said, standing back to admire the alien cupcake I had just decorated. It was Friday night, the night before the exhibit opening, and Alexis, Emma, and I were baking cupcakes at Alexis's house. Mia already left to see her dad in the city.

Emma leaned over my shoulder. "That is so cute! You should send a picture to Mia."

I wiped my hands on a towel and snapped a picture with my cell phone.

Mia texted me right back: Perfect!
Thanks! I texted back. Miss u.
Miss u 2! Have fun with George 2morrow, she wrote.
:-P, I texted.

I placed the alien cupcake in one of our plastic cupcake carriers. We invested some of our first profits in them. The cupcakes fit in little spaces in the carrier, and a lid locks on top. It helps keep the cupcakes safe—and clean—when we get them from one place to another. We had three carriers of star cupcakes and three of alien cupcakes.

It's always a satisfying feeling when the cupcakes are all done and the carriers are neatly stacked. Emma and I got to work washing and drying the dishes while Alexis went over the checklist.

"We've got the display, six dozen cupcakes, plates, and napkins," she said. "Can you guys get here by nine thirty?"

"No problem," Emma said.

"Ditto," I added.

"My mom will drive us. We can load the minivan and get to the museum by ten, so we can be all set up by the time the museum opens at eleven," Alexis said.

I looked around at Alexis's clean kitchen and realized I was calm. "I'm starting to think this is going to go all right," I said.

"Of course it is," Alexis said.

❁

117

And things did go all right—but first they went all wrong. I guess I should explain.

Mom dropped me off at Alexis's house the next morning. I wanted to look nice for the event, so instead of my usual jeans (most of which have frosting stains on them), I wore a denim skirt with dark-blue tights and ballet flats to go with the theme, and of course my official Cupcake Club T-shirt that Mia designed.

I also brought my cupcake first-aid kit, which I started carrying when we go to jobs. I saw a baker do this on a food show once, and it seemed like a good idea. I have an extra icing spreader and extra toppings and writing gel and stuff, in case any of the cupcakes needed to be touched up a bit. It comes in handy, especially when we do fancy events, like bridal showers, where the client wants every single detail to be perfect.

Alexis already had the car loaded when I got there, and Emma was walking up, yawning sleepily. Alexis's mom, Mrs. Becker, came out of the house holding a cup of coffee in one hand. Her short cropped hair was neat and gleaming as always, and she wore a crisp white skirt, a blue collared shirt, and white sneakers. She always has a lot of energy, no matter what time of day.

"Let's get you to the museum!" she said, and we piled into the minivan and buckled up. Mrs. Becker headed downtown, but we didn't get far. When we got to River Street, there was a detour. I looked out the window and saw runners wearing numbers jogging by.

"Oh, that must be the hospital charity run," I said. "I think Mr. Green is doing that."

"Don't worry, I'll just take the detour," said Mrs. Becker, making the right turn.

But the detour was backed up with lots of cars, stuck at a light. We had to wait and wait. I watched as the dashboard's digital clock kept slowly moving forward: 9:56, 9:57, 9:58.

"We're going to be late!" I said, starting to sweat a little. This was not the impression I wanted to make on Mrs. Martinez.

"Mom, is there another route?" I could tell that Alexis was anxious too. Being late for a job can be bad for business.

"Just be patient, honey, we're almost there."

We finally got to the light and arrived at the museum at 10:05. I quickly ripped off my seat belt and ran to the back of the van, opening the hatch. I had my cupcake kit in my right hand, and I picked up two carriers, kind of balancing them in my arms.

"Katie, maybe you should just take one," Emma suggested.

"No, I got it," I said. "We're running late. We need to get set up fast."

I didn't wait for the others, but hurried inside as fast as I could. Luckily, a mom held the door open for me, so I easily got inside and headed for the party room. Mrs. Martinez intercepted me by the doorway.

"There you are!" she said. Over the top of the carrier, I noticed she had on a dark-blue shirt and a big necklace with stars on it, which looked really cool.

"Hi, Mrs. Martinez," I said, hurrying past her. "We had to take a detour because of the charity run, but we will definitely have the cupcakes all set up by eleven. Don't worry."

"I wasn't worried," she said, smiling.

I walked into the party room, where George's little brothers were chasing each other (which is all they seem to do, right? They must be having fun). Anyway, I had to kind of lean to the side to avoid one of them, when the top carrier I was carrying started to slide off.

"No . . . nooooo!" I yelled.

What happened next felt like it happened in

120

slow motion. I watched in horror as the carrier fell out of my arms. Luckily, I was right by the table, so the carrier didn't have far to fall. But it landed upside down.

My stomach sank. I carefully placed the bottom carrier and my cupcake kit on the table. Then I slowly turned over the fallen carrier, and I could see that the inside of the plastic lid was smeared with blue icing. Not good.

"Katie, what happened?" Emma asked, her blue eyes wide. She and Alexis had caught up to me.

"I'm so sorry," I said, my eyes filling with tears. "It tipped over." I lifted up the lid and almost cried when I saw that the once-beautiful space cupcakes were now a big, blue mess.

"You brought your kit, right?" Alexis asked. "We can fix them."

I shook my head. "See how most of the stars are smeared with blue? There's no way to fix that."

I was about to cry when George ran up. "Whoa! What'd you do now, Silly Arms?"

For the first time ever, it hurt my feelings when George said that. I felt embarrassed and stupid and angry. But then something happened. An image of the Silly Arms sprinkler popped into my head. . . . Sprinkler . . .

121

"Wait," I said. "I think I know what to do."

I opened my cupcake kit and took out the icing spreader and a jar of silver sprinkles.

"We can fix this," I said. "Let's take off the stars that are totally covered and leave the good ones. We can smooth out the icing as best as we can and then sprinkle the silver glitter on top. It'll look like . . . space dust!"

"Silver glitter definitely looks spacey," Emma agreed. "That's a great idea."

"Can you and Emma fix the cupcakes, so Mom and I can get the display set up?" Alexis asked, and I nodded.

"I can help," George offered.

"Thanks," I said, and I wasn't mad at him anymore. "Alexis will show you what to do."

Emma and I got to work fixing the cupcakes. It was messy, but in the end the cupcakes came out looking really nice. When we finished we carefully placed them on the rocket ship display.

"Katie, I think it looks even better with the sparkles!" Emma said as she admired the sparkling cupcakes.

I stood back and looked at the display. "You know, maybe it does!"

Alexis started stacking up the empty carriers.

122

"Come on, we've got to get these back to the car and clean up."

We finished just in time for the exhibit opening, and Alexis took some pictures of it to add to the photo book we show our clients. Then Mrs. Martinez gathered all the kids and their parents together in front of a curtain blocking the exhibit room.

"Presenting the new space exhibit at the Maple Grove Children's Museum!" she announced. "I'm going to give you a brief tour of the new features, and then you're all welcome to join us for cupcakes in the party room."

She nodded to George, who dramatically pulled aside the curtain. Everyone oohed and aahed all at once. The exhibit looked awesome, even better than the picture Mrs. Martinez had showed us. Giant planets hung from the star-covered ceiling, and the big rocket ship looked totally awesome, with a shiny blue body, red fins, and light-up buttons going up the sides.

While Mrs. Martinez gave the tour, we went back to the party room to get ready for the guests.

"She asked us to hand out the cupcakes, so the kids aren't grabbing for them," Alexis said, so we got the plates and napkins ready to hand out with the cupcakes.

A few minutes later we heard a rousing cheer, and then a mob of kids ran through the doorway. They screeched to a halt at the sound of Alexis's voice.

"One at a time, people! One at a time! There are enough cupcakes for everybody," she yelled.

I giggled. "You sound like Ms. Chen." Our gym teacher is great at barking out orders.

"That's what I was going for," Alexis explained. "She knows how to get kids to do things."

The next twenty minutes was a cupcake frenzy as we handed out cupcake after cupcake. The kids ate them superfast and then ran back into the museum.

George walked up to me, munching on an alien cupcake. "These are so good!" he said. "And they look so cool."

"Thanks," I said. "Mia designed them. I wish she was here. This is so much fun."

"I have an idea," George said. He looked over at Alexis and Emma. "Everybody grab a cupcake and follow me."

George took us to the exhibit, which was crawling with kids.

"Step aside, step aside, please," he told the kids on the rocket. "We have an important photo opportunity here."

Then he gestured to us. "Okay, climb up."

Alexis, Emma, and I looked at one another. Were we really going to do this?

"Why not?" I said, and I started to climb up the rocket, holding a cupcake in one hand. Alexis and Emma followed, and soon all three of us were hanging from the sides of the ship.

George held up his phone. "Okay, guys, look at me and say 'cheese.'"

"You mean 'green cheese,'" Emma corrected him.

"No," I said. "It's 'cupcakes . . . in . . . spaaaaaace!'"

We all laughed, and George took the picture and texted it to me. In the subject line he put, "Silly Arms in Space," but I didn't mind. I might have silly arms, but at least I fixed the cupcakes!

CHAPTER 18

Sprinkles & Surprises

$\mathcal{I}$ was pretty relieved that everything went well at the children's museum, but my worries were not over for the day. I still had to meet Jeff and his daughter, Emily, at the pizza place. I wanted to make a good impression, so I kept on my skirt and tights, but I changed out of my cupcake T-shirt (which had splotches of blue frosting on it, anyway) and into a blue striped shirt that I have.

"You look nice," Mom said when I came down the stairs.

"So do you," I said. Normally, she dresses up when she goes out with Jeff, but today she was wearing a brand-new red short-sleeved sweater and a really cute flowered skirt. "Do you want to make a good impression too?"

Mom laughed. "Honestly, I'm nervous too, Katie. I met Emily once, but it was just for a little while. It's important to me that she ... well, that she thinks I'm nice."

"Well, you are nice," I said. "The nicest mom ever. So that shouldn't be a problem."

Mom hugged me. "And you are the nicest daughter ever."

"So I guess we have nothing to worry about," I said, but inside I wasn't quite convinced yet.

Instead of Jeff picking us up, Mom and I drove to Vinnie's Pizza, which is right in town. The brick restaurant looks small in front, but when you walk in, you see rows and rows of tables that go all the way back to the counter and to the open kitchen where the cooks work. You can see the guys throwing the dough up into the air, which is really cool. I have tried throwing pizza dough in the air when we make it at home, but I can never get a perfect circle. And once it ended up on the ceiling fan. (Don't ask!)

We parked on the street, and when we walked up to Vinnie's, Jeff and Emily were standing there. She looked just like her picture, with long brown hair and brown eyes. She was wearing a skirt too, and I briefly wondered if she was also trying to

127

make a good impression or if she just liked skirts.

Jeff gave Mom a kiss on the cheek. "Hello," he said. "Katie, this is Emily. Emily, this is Katie."

"Hi," Emily and I said at the same time, both shyly. Then we kind of just looked at each other. *Awkward!*

"Let's get a table," Mom said quickly, sensing the mood, and we went inside.

We quickly walked across the black-and-white checkerboard floor to a table along the wall. Mom and I sat on one side and Jeff and Emily sat on the other, so Mom was across from Jeff, and Emily and I were staring at each other.

"I'm glad you suggested Vinnie's. This is Emily's favorite pizza place too," Jeff said. "Right, Emily?"

Emily nodded. "Yeah, the veggie pizza is really good."

"It is," I agreed, and from the corner of my eye I could see Mom beaming. I knew what she was probably thinking. *They like the same pizza! They're going to get along!*

But Emily and I didn't say much after that. Jeff and Mom were doing all the talking.

"I'm so hungry, I could eat two whole pizzas!" Jeff said. "That hospital run took a lot of energy. Right, Emily?"

Emily nodded again.

"Katie had a busy day too, at the children's museum," Mom reported. "Wasn't it busy there, Katie?"

I nodded. It was like Mom and Jeff were trying to have our conversation for us. Thankfully, the waitress came over.

"What can I get for you guys?" she asked.

"How about two veggie pizzas?" Jeff suggested.

"And a salad," Mom added.

"And garlic knots," Emily piped up.

"And chicken fingers," I added, and then we all laughed.

Jeff shook his head. "Wow, I guess we're all hungry!"

The waitress left the table, and after laughing like that, things seemed a little less awkward.

"Emily loves to bake too," Jeff said. "Right, Emily?"

"Yeah," Emily said shyly. "I saw some pictures of the cupcakes you do on your website. Where do you get your ideas for decorations? That's my favorite part of baking."

"Then you would love my friend Mia," I said. "She is really artistic, and she comes up with a lot of our designs for us. I guess it runs in the family.

Her mom is a fashion stylist. She always dresses like she's a model herself."

Emily's eyes got wide. "Wow, really? You have cool friends."

That made me feel kind of proud. But it's true! I do have cool friends.

"So, what school do you go to?" I asked.

"Hamilton," Emily replied, and I was surprised.

"No way!" I said. "I went there." But then I remembered Mom said Emily lived in the same town as us, so it made sense. "Is Mr. Hadler still the custodian? He was so nice."

"I know!" Emily agreed. "Once, in second grade, I got lost on the way to the library and he helped me. And he always sings those funny songs."

I laughed, and then I remembered I had an assignment from Alexis.

"So, the Cupcake Club was wondering if you had ideas for other light cupcakes," I said. "So we can build up our selection."

"Sure," Jeff said. "I'll make a list for you and get together some recipes. Then maybe you can come over and help Emily and me whip up some test cupcakes."

"Great," I said, and I knew Alexis would be really happy.

Then our food came, and we didn't talk much, but mostly because we were eating and not because things were awkward. Actually, things felt really normal, which was nice.

When we stepped outside of Vinnie's after dinner, it was dark out, but bright streetlights lit up the sidewalk.

"You know," I said, "King Cone is right down the street."

I will use any opportunity to get ice cream. But part of me didn't want the night to end, not just yet.

"After all that food?" Mom asked with a groan. But Jeff looked interested.

"Well, we did burn a lot of calories today. . . ."

"Yay!" Emily said, and that settled it. We walked to the ice-cream parlor. It's the kind where you line up outside to get your ice cream.

"What'll it be?" Jeff asked as we walked up to the window.

"A vanilla and chocolate twist cone, with lots of rainbow sprinkles," I said.

The girl behind the counter heard me, and she disappeared and quickly reappeared with the cone in her hand. There were so many sprinkles that I couldn't even see the ice cream underneath. Perfect!

"Can I have the same?" Emily asked.

"That looks good," Jeff said. "I think I'll get one too."

"Me too," Mom said.

Soon we were all holding our very sprinkly ice-cream cones.

"Wow, they really sprinkled on the sprinkles," Jeff joked.

"I love a sprinkling of sprinkles!" Mom added, and they both cracked up. I looked at Emily, and we rolled our eyes at each other.

"Let's take a walk," Jeff suggested.

We didn't get far when we saw Olivia Allen with her mom and dad.

"Mr. Green!" Olivia shouted. And then she gave me this curious look, like she was trying to figure out the scene.

"Hi, Olivia," Jeff said pleasantly. Then he held out his hand to Olivia's parents. "Hello, Mr. and Mrs. Allen. I'm Olivia's math teacher."

"Oh, *that* Mr. Green!" said Olivia's mother. "Olivia talks about you all the time. I used to be a teacher too. But when we moved here, Olivia was adamant that I not teach at her school. She said she'd be too embarrassed. So I became a tutor instead."

Jeff laughed. "Well, I try not to embarrass anyone

too much," he said with a wink at Emily.

Olivia turned red, and then I saw her looking at my mom, sizing her up. I was glad my mom looked really pretty.

"Well, nice to meet you," Jeff said, "but we've got to get moving before our cones melt."

We continued down the street. "Ugh, she's so annoying," I complained when they were out of earshot.

"Now, Katie," Mom said in a warning tone.

"No, actually, she's pretty bad," Jeff said, and I must have had a totally surprised look on my face because Jeff smiled at me and then shrugged.

"Are most of the kids in middle school annoying?" Emily wanted to know.

"No, they're mostly nice," I promised her. "You'll probably make a lot of new friends. I did."

Emily asked me a lot more questions about middle school, and Mom and Jeff were talking about a new recipe Mom was going to try, and it was all kind of nice.

I was still thinking about what Jeff said about Olivia. That was surprising, that adults could see kids as real people like that. And the fact that Emily was coming to middle school soon—that was surprising too.

I guess you could say the last few weeks have been sprinkled with lots of surprises. Some bad, but mostly good, and in the end, I was left with a lot of pretty colors all mixed together, and that was the best thing of all. Because everyone knows sprinkles make everyone happy. Especially rainbow ones.

Want another sweet cupcake?
Here's a sneak peek
of the eighteenth book in the

CUPCaKe🧁DIaRIeS

series:

Mia
fashion plates
and cupcakes

Mia

We Are Such Pros!

"Do you need help with those, Katie?" I asked.

My friend Katie was carrying two cupcake carriers stacked on top of each other, and a bag of supplies dangled from her wrist. It made me a little nervous watching her. Katie is my BFF here in Maple Grove and I love her, but she's had some serious cupcake disasters before.

"No, I got it," Katie assured me. She carefully placed the carriers on our cupcake sales table and then looked around. "Wow, there's some cool stuff here."

We were inside the Maple Grove Women's Club, which may not sound super exciting, except that it was the day of their craft fair. Local artists and craftspeople were setting up tables with the stuff they'd made, like knitted scarves and handmade beaded jewelry.

"Yeah, I hope we can look around a little," I said. "Alexis was really smart to suggest we set up here."

At that moment my friend Alexis walked up to us, carrying a notebook and a cash box.

"Did I just hear you say I was really smart?" she asked with a grin.

I nodded. "I never would have thought to sell cupcakes at a craft fair, but it's kind of a genius idea."

"Not genius, just obvious," Alexis said. "People who go to craft fairs get hungry. Besides, our cupcakes are handmade too, and they're like little works of art. I think the decorations and flavors you guys came up with are genius."

"Thanks," I said. I was pretty proud of what we had done. "We should get things set up before it starts."

My mom is a member of the Women's Club, so I had arrived early with her and started to set up the table. Once Alexis had suggested we sell at the craft fair, we came up with a theme: Crafty Cupcakes.

Whenever we do an event, we have to plan out a bunch of things: what flavor to make the cup-cakes, how to decorate the cupcakes, how to display the cupcakes, and how to decorate the table. For the craft fair, I thought we should stick with what people think of as traditional "cupcakey" colors— pink, mint green, light blue, and yellow. So the first thing I did was put down a pink tablecloth. We had used it for a baby shower once, and we like to reuse things to help with the costs.

Then I set up a backdrop, which I made from one of those big trifold cardboard displays that you can get for school projects. For the middle panel, I cut out letters from scrapbook paper to spell out "Crafty Cupcakes." The papers had little white flowers and dots on them, so it looked really cute. Then I had drawn some pictures of cupcakes along with pictures of crafty things, like paintbrushes and yarn and knitting needles.

On each side panel, I had printed out our Cupcake Club logo: a cupcake in a light blue wrapper with pink icing and a red cherry on top, and the words "cupcake" above it and "club" below. I had designed the logo myself at summer camp. We made T-shirts with the logo, too, which we wore whenever we had a cupcake event. Anyway, I stood up the backdrop at the back of the table, and then I was ready for the cupcake displays.

It's tempting to buy cool new stuff for our

displays each time, but then we wouldn't make as much profit. And Alexis is always talking about profit since that's the money we get to keep. So we reuse what we can or make what we need. For this display, I bought some wooden cake stands from the craft store and painted them in our cupcakey colors. Then I added a clear, shiny coat so that it would be safe to put food on the stands. They looked really pretty on the table.

"I'll get the rest of the cupcakes from the car," Katie said, hurrying off.

"Mind if I set up the cash box?" Alexis asked.

"That's fine, I've got this," I said.

I slipped on some thin plastic gloves and opened up the first carrier. It contained our first batch of cupcakes: vanilla cake with vanilla icing, decorated with flowers made of fondant. Fondant is this paste made of sugar that you can roll out like dough and cut into shapes. We'd used pink and yellow for the flowers, so I put them on the green cake stand for a nice contrast.

The second carrier held our "yarn" cupcakes. We'd made red velvet cupcakes with cream cheese frosting. Then we'd used marzipan, which is a sugary almond paste that you can shape into stuff—kind of like edible modeling clay. We'd dyed it blue and then rolled it into little balls of "yarn," to go with the crafts theme. The yarn looked really cute sitting on top of the icing. I put those on the pink cake stand.

Katie came in carrying more cupcake carriers. The third held chocolate cupcakes with chocolate frosting. We'd decorated them with little jelly candies that we thought looked like jewels. For our fourth kind of cupcake, we had gone with one of our more adventurous flavors—lemon ginger, because a lot of people will buy a cupcake if it's a flavor they've never tried before. We'd topped them with pale-yellow lemon frosting and decorated them with birds.

I think I was most proud of the bird cupcakes, because I had experimented a lot to find the best way to do them. You know those old-fashioned candies that are shaped like leaves? I thought they kind of looked like birds bodies. So I'd sliced them through the middle to make them thinner. Then I'd used little tubes of icing to draw on an eye, a beak, and wings, and I'd made swirly designs all around them. They looked really amazing.

Katie helped me put the rest of the cupcakes on the stands, and then we stashed the carriers under the table. Alexis, Katie, and I stood in front of the table to see how everything looked.

"This might be our nicest display yet," Alexis remarked. "It's too bad Emma is not here."

Emma, the fourth member of the Cupcake Club, was off on a modeling job in the city.

"I'll send her a picture," Katie said, taking out her phone.

Alexis scrolled through the screen on her own smartphone. "So, display, check. Cupcakes, check. Business cards, check. Cash box, check. Flyers, check." She looked up at us. "Wow, I can't believe it. I think we're all set. We didn't forget anything."

I checked the time. "There's a few minutes before the doors open. I want to look around before it gets busy."

"I'll watch the table," Alexis offered.

"Thanks," Katie said. "I want to look around too."

So Katie and I walked around the room, checking out the crafts. Some of the stuff was kind of old-fashioned and looked like my grandma would like it, but some of it was really cool. We went to a table with beaded jewelry first, and Katie picked up a bracelet made out of chunky glass beads.

"This is so cool! The beads look like candy, almost," she said.

The woman setting up the booth smiled. "I

call that my 'candy shop' style," she said, and then nodded to our shirts. "So, you're the girls from the cupcake stand?"

We nodded. "Yes," I said. "We started a cupcake club at school and turned it into a business."

"That's really ambitious," she said. "Good luck today!"

We thanked her and moved on to a table full of knitted scarves and then to another cool table with all these awesome animals and creatures sewn from felt. The girl behind it looked like she was in high school, and her blond hair was streaked with red and purple.

"These are sooo cute!" Katie squealed, picking up a little green squirrel with a goofy face.

"That's my favorite one," the girl said.

Katie dug into her jeans pocket and pulled out some bills. "I have to get this. You're coming home with me, Nutsy."

I laughed. "Nutsy?"

"Well, she's a squirrel, isn't she? And squirrels like nuts," Katie said.

"I think it's a good name for a squirrel," said the girl, giving Katie her change. She also handed over a business card with the name Super Stuffies on it.

Then I noticed people were starting to come

through the doors, so I tapped Katie on the arm.

"We'd better go help Alexis," I said.

When we got back to the table I saw a glamorous-looking woman with long black hair standing there. She wore black skinny jeans, black boots, and a black short-sleeved turtleneck. For a second I didn't recognize her.

"Hi, Mom," I said, running up to her. My mom always looks glamorous, whether she's at the supermarket or going to eat at a hot restaurant in the city. You've always got to look good when you're a fashion stylist.

"Mia, the table looks lovely," Mom said. "You girls did a wonderful job."

"They certainly did."

A gray-haired woman walked up to us. She wore a long, flowy purple tunic over black leggings, which made her look very artistic.

"Mia, this is Mrs. Barrows, the president of the Women's Club," my mom said. "This my daughter and her friends Katie and Alexis."

Mrs. Barrows looked over the cupcake booth. "This is a lovely addition to our craft fair. I can't believe you girls made these cupcakes yourselves. They're beautiful!"

Alexis took a vanilla flower cupcake from the

stand. "They taste as good as they look," she said, handing her one.

"Why, thank you!" Mrs. Barrows said. She unwrapped it and took a bite. "You're certainly right. This is delicious! You girls are quite professional."

Then two women walked up to our table, and we had to go into "sales mode," as Alexis would say. Katie and I answered questions about what was in each cupcake, and Alexis took the money, made change, and made sure everyone left with a business card and a flyer.

It was kind of a long day. We were pretty much busy the whole time, and we took turns leaving the table to eat the bagged lunches we had brought. Things finally slowed down in the afternoon.

Alex put her hands on her hips, surveying the table. We had about two dozen cupcakes left. She looked around the room, counting.

"We should give one to each of the vendors," she said finally. "I don't think we'll sell out, and these are the kind of people who appreciate homemade things."

I'm always amazed by Alexis. It's like her mind is constantly churning out great business ideas.

"Let's do it," I agreed, and we took turns going to the tables and giving a cupcake to each vendor—along with a business card, of course. Everyone was really happy to get a cupcake.

We even had time to do a little shopping by the end of the day. I bought a really cool crocheted infinity scarf with black fringe along the edges, and when Katie wasn't looking, I went back to the jewelry table and got her the bracelet that looked like candy. I figured I'd save it for her birthday.

I also went back to the girl with the stuffies. One of her creatures was a little purple monster, and I thought Ethan might like it. He's the mostly-annoying-but-sometimes-cute son of Lynne, my dad's girlfriend.

"No charge," the girl said when I tried to pay. "That was an awesome cupcake."

"Wow, thank you," I said. "That's really nice of you."

When I got back to the table, Alexis was counting out the cash box.

"Except for the cupcakes we gave away, we sold them all," she said, looking at the clock, "with only five minutes to go. That's pretty perfect."

"Definitely," Katie agreed.

"Mrs. Barrows said we were professional," I reminded them. "Maybe she's right. I mean, it's like we've figured out how to smooth away all the problems we usually have. We are awesome!"

"This *was* a pretty smooth event," Alexis agreed, "but there are always going to be problems. That's just the way it is in a business."

"Maybe," I said. "But I'll keep my fingers crossed that things stay smooth."

Little did I know that things were about to get bumpier than lumpy cupcake frosting—but it wasn't the Cupcake Club's fault at all.

All About Katie!

Katie is going through a lot of changes in her life. Have you been paying attention? How well do you know Katie? Take this quiz and find out!

(If you don't want to write in your book, use a separate piece of paper.)

1. Katie's last name is
   A. Jones
   B. Smith
   C. Brown
   D. Blue

2. Katie's best friend is
   A. Mia
   B. Alexis
   C. Emma
   D. Olivia

3. True or false: Katie is very athletic.
   A. True
   B. False

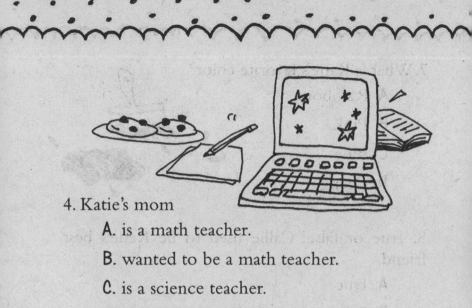

4. Katie's mom

    A. is a math teacher.

    B. wanted to be a math teacher.

    C. is a science teacher.

    D. is dating a math teacher.

5. Who is Katie's crush?

    A. George

    B. Jake

    C. Matt

    D. Chris

6. What is Katie's nickname?

    A. Spaghetti legs

    B. Silly arms

    C. Puppy face

    D. Bunny

7. What is Katie's favorite color?

    A. Rainbow

    B. Pink

    C. Blue

    D. Orange

8. True or false: Callie used to be Katie's best friend.

    A. True

    B. False

☆ ☆ ☆ **Did you get the right answers?** ☆ ☆

1. C 2. A 3. B 4. D 5. A 6. B 7. A 8. A

How did you do?

7–8 correct: Wow, you can be one of Katie's BFFs!

5–6 correct: Not bad, but you need to pay a little more attention.

3–4 correct: That's not a good score. You owe Katie an apology!

1–2 correct: You need to try again and do better—or you'll be forced to eat lunch with Olivia Allen forever!

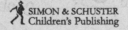

Still Hungry?
There's always room for another Cupcake!

Katie and the
Cupcake Cure
1

Mia in the Mix
2

Emma on Thin Icing
3

Alexis and the
Perfect Recipe
4

Katie, Batter Up!
5

Mia's Baker's Dozen
6

Emma All Stirred Up!
7

Alexis
Cool as a Cupcake
8

Katie and the
Cupcake War
9

Want more

CUPCaKe🧁DIARIES?

Visit **CupcakeDiariesBooks.com**
for the series trailer, excerpts, activities,
and everything you need for throwing
your own cupcake party!

Coco Simon always dreamed of opening a cupcake bakery but was afraid she would eat all of the profits. When she's not daydreaming about cupcakes, Coco edits children's books and has written close to one hundred books for children, tweens, and young adults, which is a lot less than the number of cupcakes she's eaten. Cupcake Diaries is the first time Coco has mixed her love of cupcakes with writing.

You're never too young to change the world!

These second graders in North carolina fundraised to sponsor one year of school for Jarana in Nepal!

GOAL Getters
Global Opportunities, Awareness, Leadership
little leaders making a BIG Difference

They're changing the world. You can too with:

GOAL Getters!

With **GOAL Getters** in the classroom, you will:

* Learn how to be a leader in your community
* Host creative fundraisers like bake sales!
* Give girls the opportunity to go to school!

Talk to your teacher and visit
shesthefirst.org/GOALGetters

GOAL Getters
Global Opportunities, Awareness, Leadership

She's the First